CASSIE MINT

Mail Order Mountain: The Complete Series

BLACK CHERRY

PUBLISHING

Contents

I

Grizzly Beard

Description

I

'm a mountain man's mail order bride.

But I'm knocking on the wrong cabin door.

Moving out here to start my life from scratch—that's scary enough. But then the world's surliest man finds me on his deck, and it's about to get a whole lot worse.

He thinks I should scurry back to the city. *I* think he's a big, bearded jerk. He still agrees to take me to my fiance, though.

But a fallen tree makes us stop for the night. And huddling for warmth... turns out that's no myth after all.

I wake up in a huge muddle, my cheek resting on a big, strong chest.

...I'm doomed. I've fallen for the wrong mountain man.

Luna

Okay, don't make fun of me, but I've been practicing my knock. First impressions are a big deal, you know? And even though I've been emailing back and forth with Aiden McRae for months now, I want to get this exactly right.

You only get one chance to be like, 'Tadaa! I'm your mail order bride!", after all.

In my head, I was gonna be cool and collected. My clothes would be spotless and unrumpled, and I'd smile nice and wide, and Aiden would fall in love with me in a heartbeat. A chorus of birds would break into song, and he'd pick me up and spin me around in his big, strong arms.

Whatever he looks like. Kinda hard to picture it without knowing that.

Of course, I didn't count on the half mile trek to this cabin up from the road, lugging my suitcase and sewing machine over a carpet of pine needles and wet rocks. And didn't realize I'm so freaking behind on my cardio, either—I'm red-faced and sweating like a sinner in church. If my husband-to-be picks me up right now, I'll probably squelch.

"Shoot. Come on, Luna."

I blow the wild strands of hair out of my face and smooth down my favorite lavender dress with trembling hands. There's no need to be this nervous.

I mean, sure, my whole future is on the line, and maybe my only chance at love. But the mail order people know what they're doing, and I'm 99.9% sure that they wouldn't let a serial killer sign up.

My breath fogs in the cold air as I stumble back a few steps, peering up at the cabin. Buying time? Maybe. But I want a good look at my new home, too.

It's understated, this cabin. Strong and sturdy and well crafted, made with the kind of wood that blends into the landscape. A deck wraps around the outside, and a hatchet and pile of cut logs are tucked under a wood shed against a side wall. The windows are shadowed.

It must have rained here in the last hour or so. The air's extra fresh, scented with petrichor and damp soil, and there are still droplets clinging to the glass window panes.

It's so *austere*. Nothing like my playful apartment back in the city, with my polka dot welcome mat and my navy bedroom curtains printed with the phases of the moon. You can tell a Man lives here, and not just a Man, but a Manly Man. One who speaks in grunts and knows how to skin a deer.

Maybe this is a huge mistake. I stumble back another step, my heart hammering. If I get my bags back down the mountain and call the local cab company from the road—

The door wrenches open, replaced immediately with a pair of broad, plaid-covered shoulders. A bearded man glares down at me from inside the cabin, thick eyebrows lowered over dark eyes, and he looms so high above me that my knees wobble.

"Um," I squeak. "Aiden?"

The frown deepens. "Wrong cabin," the man rumbles.

Thank. Freaking. God.

We didn't swap photos as part of the mail order program. It's one of the reasons I chose Soulmate Express—I didn't want any *judge 'em by their looks,* swipe right shenanigans. I want love. Soulful love.

And even though I'm still clueless about my future husband, I'm glad he's not this grumpy Goliath. Bullet: dodged.

"Oh. Right. Could you point me toward Aiden McRae's cabin, please?"

The man says nothing. He's silent and brooding, those dark eyes running over my rumpled clothes and bright cheeks, my messed up hair and nervous smile, then to the luggage stacked on the deck behind me.

I didn't think it was possible for this man to scowl even more, but here it is. He looks ready to roar like a bear. Damn, I didn't mean to encroach on his territory or whatever. Hopefully I didn't accidentally scent-mark any trees.

"Actually." The deck creaks as I back up, my voice unnaturally bright. "Forget it. I've already disturbed you enough, sir. I'll just get out of your—" *beard* "—um, hair, and call a cab from the road. Sorry. Sorry."

My fingers scrabble at the handles on my cases. Heat burns on my cheeks, and I can't get away from here fast enough. Who cares if it rains again? But then—

"Stop."

The low order makes me freeze. I blink at the man through my blonde hair.

He sighs and says, "It's not safe to go alone. Aiden McRae's on the other side of the mountain."

Ah, crap. I'm that lost? Freaking cab driver. Why did I tip him so well? Did he drop me off at the wrong cabin on purpose?

What if they're some kind of serial killer duo, where the driver leaves unsuspecting women on this man's deck like gift-wrapped treats? What if this is all some nefarious plan and that hatchet isn't for logs after all? What if—

"I'll drive you." The man ducks through the doorway, finally stepping out into the mountain air, and my stomach swoops. Beneath the beard and the scowl and the general cloud of irritation, this man is… he's…

I think the word is *rugged.*

"Um." I clear my throat, suddenly dazed. "Thank you."

He's square-jawed and handsome. Maybe a decade older than me, but his dark hair is thick and his eyes crinkle at the corners. Like he's been squinting into the sun his whole life, and sunglasses never even crossed his manly mind.

The wood creaks beneath his bulk as he tugs the door closed and comes to pick up my cases. He lifts them as easily as if they were stuffed with feather pillows, which, believe me, they are not. My sewing machine alone weighs more than I do.

Could he lift me with one hand, too?

Not helpful, Luna. Jeez.

"My truck's back down near the road. You gonna be okay in those shoes?"

I peer down at my gray suede ankle boots, already ruined by the slog up the mountainside. Stray pine needles have stuck to the soaked fabric, and there's a soggy dark tideline around the tops of my feet. "Yeah. I'm good."

"Alright, stay close. The animals get bolder around dusk."

They do?

What kinds of animals? Like cute, fluffy bunnies, right?

A mournful howl drifts through the trees, and I shiver. Sounds like it came from far away—but not far enough. Nowhere near far enough, damn it.

The man's eyes glitter with amusement as he starts the walk back down the mountainside. "Come on, city girl. Better stay close. You're the perfect snack size for a grizzly."

* * *

"I knew there'd be bears and wolves and stuff."

"Right."

"I'm just saying. I'm not completely clueless."

"'Course not." The man's mouth is a flat line, his expression as severe as ever, but somehow I *know* he's laughing at me as he loads his truck. It's a dark blue beater, kept tucked away against a rock face, and I linger extra close as that howl echoes around my brain. It's still light out, the golden sunshine bleeding through the trees, but the shadows are getting longer.

"Could you, um." I point at my sewing machine case where it lies on its side in the center of the truck bed. "Could you tie that down or something, please? It's pretty valuable."

It's my whole livelihood, but whatever. No big deal.

The amusement fades, and the man sighs as he digs out two ratchet straps from his truck cab and sets about winching my luggage down tight. I nibble on my lip, watching him work, and feel about three inches tall. Even all the way out here, starting my new life, I'm still a pain in the ass.

"Better, princess?"

I nod, throat tight, and we load into the truck cab in silence.

"Luna," I say after a while once we're bouncing along the rocky track. Trees and rocks whip past outside the windows, and squirrels scurry along branches in flashes of fur. "My name is Luna Lindgren."

I don't want this man to call me princess. The scathing way he says it, like he knows everything about me already and finds me lacking… it makes me want to cry.

"Griff."

It takes me a second to realize what he's saying. "Oh. Hey, Griff."

We swing around a bend in the road, engine rumbling and truck rocking. Surreptitiously, I check my seat belt is secure.

"So you're gonna be Luna McRae?" Every time he speaks, the low rumble of his voice takes me by surprise. It's like I can *feel* it, vibrating through my body. But hey, maybe that's the truck. "Or will you keep Lindgren?"

I glance at my driver, mortified. He knows I'm a mail order bride? Is it that obvious? I mean, it's not like I'm wandering around in a veil and bridal gown. I'm not ashamed of what I'm doing here, but I'm not exactly out to brag about it either, because what girl wants to admit that she couldn't find love the ordinary way?

I'm a die hard romantic. A big believer in fate.

And yet the dating scene back in the city… it left me cold. Cold and jaded and lonely.

"Some of the locals call this Mail Order Mountain," Griff explains, like he somehow read the emotions flitting across my face even with his eyes fixed on the road. "We get a lot of brides turning up here for a fresh start. Grooms, too. Hard to meet someone when it's just you, your cabin, and some trees."

Yeah. Aiden said as much in his emails.

"But what's your excuse?" Dark eyes flick to me, then back to the road. "No one up to your standards in the city, Luna? Or did you want the authentic mountain man experience? A man to chop wood shirtless then carry you back to his cabin? Spread you out by the fire and make you forget about all the hassles of modern life?"

Jerk.

Knotting my fingers in my lap, I glare out of the passenger window in furious silence. Did I think Griff was nice? I was wrong. So wrong. He's a judgmental asshole who thinks he knows me from one glance, and I can't wait to get far, far away from him. Aiden McRae's cabin can't come soon enough.

Spread me out by the fire. Ugh. Please.

I've never been 'spread' in my whole life. Jackass.

And the longer we go without speaking, the more pissed off I get, so there's no use for it. I clear my throat and force the words to come out evenly. "You don't know me."

Griff grunts. "I've seen it happen around here enough times. City girls swan in, looking for an exotic thrill, and within a few weeks they're gone, leaving nothing but broken hearts behind. Couldn't hack the mountain life."

Did that happen to him? Is that why he's so grouchy with me? My belly drops at the thought.

"Well, I'm not like that."

He shrugs, his grip tight on the wheel. "We'll see."

Such an ass. I frown out at the trees, their bark tinged blue in the fading light, and hate that I'm reliant on this man to get where I'm going. Hate that he's helping me out even as he judges me to hell and back.

At least it's a big mountain. Once I'm tucked up safe with

Aiden, I'll hardly ever see Griff again.

Can't wait. I'm counting the minutes. The truck lurches beneath me and I grip the door handle with a clammy hand, suddenly feeling sick.

At least when I *do* see Griff in the future, he'll know he got me all wrong. That I'm not some tourist here for a whirlwind romance; that I'm here for the long haul.

Because my heart is heavy duty. I may not have been in love before, but I know instinctively—once my heart is gone, it's *gone.*

It's been a long time waiting. Hoping and yearning.

And I sure hope Aiden is the man I've been looking for.

Griff

⁓⚬ჲ⚬⁓

The mail order programs have a lot to answer for. So many broken-hearted idiots mooning around their cabins; so many city slickers trekking out here only to discover that they prefer WiFi to romance after all. As the head of Mountain Rescue, I've dug more than my share of rental cars out of the dirt; I've saved dozens of runaway brides from winter storms. They always say the same thing: it's not how they imagined it would be.

Those dreams of romance are dangerous. Literally.

"So." Luna's voice is hoarse, but it can't be from talking. We've been bouncing along the rocky dirt track in taut silence, both staring out at the road with our jaws clenched. And I hate hearing the strain in her soft voice, hate knowing that I put it there, but what's the sense in trying to fix it?

We'll be at Aiden's cabin in less than two hours. Two hours, and then she's another man's girl to soothe.

"So," I prompt when she says nothing else. Damn me, I should know better than to take an interest, but there's

12

something about this girl that piques my curiosity.

She's beautiful, obviously, with her pale blonde hair and the glacial pools of her eyes. Those rosy cheeks and the dimples when she smiles. When I first opened the door to my cabin, my heart actually skipped a beat, and fuck, I thought that only happened in stories.

That's not it, though. Not why I can't resist wanting to know more.

Maybe it's the way hard steel filled her voice when she said *you don't know me.* Putting me in my place for being rude.

Or maybe it's the floral scent of her, filling the cab of my truck. Is that lavender?

"Tell me about Aiden McRae," Luna says, and I huff, scowling out at the road.

Do I have to? Do we really need to do this? It's bad enough that she's the first woman I've felt this strong of a pull towards in—well, ever. Bad enough that I'm delivering her to another man. Now I have to talk him up?

"He's fine."

Luna snorts, turning to me at last. Her gaze is like a warm hand coasting over my skin, and I shift in my seat. Urge the truck forward faster, heart thumping as I wrench at the wheel.

"'Fine'? Are you serious?"

Yup. "He's seriously fine."

"Griff, come on. I'm going to marry this guy."

Don't remind me. "That's on you, Luna. You must have talked with him, right? Must have figured out if you were a good fit?"

Fuck. If I'd been signed up to the mail order program, would she still have picked Aiden McRae? Or is there any chance that Luna would have chosen me? Would we have talked for a few months, moving from shy chatting to deeper confessions? When I opened the door to my cabin, would Luna have been on the right deck after all?

Trees whip past the window, faster and faster, and I force myself to press the brakes and go slower. No sense driving like an idiot just because there's a pool of acid spreading through my chest.

Maybe I should sign up for Soulmate Express after all, dangers of romance be damned. God knows I don't want to bump into Luna and Aiden down at Cloudy Lake and be the loner. Always watching and wanting. Sighing after another man's wife like a creep.

Except—no. There's no point in signing up, and I squeeze the steering wheel until my knuckles creak. Every breath I suck down is laced with lavender.

The girl I want is already matched up. I'm too late.

"Aiden's..."

What? Am I gonna ruin this for one of the best guys on the mountain? Am I gonna make Luna unhappy just because I'm a jealous ass?

"Aiden's a good man. You'll like him, princess."

Don't know if that's what she wants to hear, but I guess we're done talking again. There's a soft sigh, and then she stares back out of the window. Mouth pursed, Luna watches the dying light fade away between the trees; the shadows lengthen and pool together on the forest floor as stars wink between the branches.

I wait for the usual comments. The freaked out whispers that it's so dark here, and creepy at night, and it gets so cold, and she had no idea in the city that this would feel so remote. That maybe we should head down off the mountain to the nearest town right this second.

I wait, but the complaints and escape plans don't come.

So perhaps I misjudged Luna Lindgren. But as we wind along the mountain path to her fiance, it doesn't make me feel better. Not at all.

* * *

The road along the mountainside is treacherous at the best of times. Prone to rock slips and flooding, to fallen trees and wayward cars half in ditches, and I trust this road about as much as a hungry bear in springtime.

Shouldn't have tried to drive it at night, not really. But I took one look at Luna and my instincts started screaming to get her away from me, to put some distance between us, else I'd do something unwise. Something like try to get closer. Something like admit to this *hunger* for her gnawing on my ribs.

"Not far now," I tell her, and I'm not sure which of us I'm trying to soothe. "An hour or so, then you'll be tucked up with Aiden."

"Spread out by the fire," Luna says dryly, and I wince. Yeah, that was a dick thing to say. "Will you be okay driving back alone in the dark?"

"Sure." Me, I'm used to the wilderness. Prepared. It's a lot less scary than the petite young woman sitting in my passenger seat.

The second I have that thought, we round a bend in the road and I slam on the brakes. A huge tree lies across the road, thick trunk digging a rut into the dirt. Branches are splayed everywhere on one side; tangled roots wave at the stars on the other, clumps of dirt still clinging to the bark.

"Fuck," I say to no one. "*Fuck*."

Why am I surprised? Things like this happen on this road. It was always a risk coming out here tonight, and now I've set Luna up for a cold, miserable night.

"Princess…"

"Don't call me that," Luna snaps, and I swallow. Yeah, this is gonna be hell.

"Sorry. I should've—should've thought before I drove you all the way out here. If we back up half a mile, there's another path to Aiden's cabin, but it's worse than this one. We shouldn't drive it in the dark. I can take you back to my cabin, but reversing can be tricky—"

"It's fine." Luna pulls her legs up and wraps her arms around her shins. "What would you normally do, Griff?"

Sleep here for the night. There's no way I'm suggesting that, though.

But: "Stay here?" she asks, like she can read my mind.

"Well…"

"Do you have blankets?"

Obviously. I have everything we need and more. But Luna's gonna be cold and stiff and uncomfortable, and she's clearly not my biggest fan. Fuck, I hate that. I'd give anything to change it. And it's a gamble, but there's a chance I could get her back to my cabin tonight; could build her a fire and warm up some hot soup.

"Griff." Luna's voice is soft. "Do you have supplies?"

"Yeah."

"Then we'll stay here."

"But…"

"But what?" The steel is back, snapping through her tone.

Luna's staring at me through the gloom, her pale blue eyes ghostly in the moonlight. "But you think I can't hack a single night without a feather bed? You think I'm going to complain all night and keep you awake?"

"No." I really don't think those things. I just…

I want to do right by her. That's all.

And on a selfish level, can I last a whole night in a truck cab with her? I'm not sure. Not for the reasons she thinks, but because every breath of her lavender scent erodes another piece of my self control. Every word in her soft voice digs deeper into my chest.

But Luna's staring at me like she's waiting for the worst. Like she's bracing for me to be a dick to her again. And I can't do that, can't disappoint her like that, so I clear my throat and nod.

"We'll sleep here tonight. Then I'll back up the truck at first light, and we'll take the other path to Aiden's cabin. Okay?"

There's a long, slow inhale, then cool fingertips ghost across my shoulder. I stiffen, heart pounding, until they drop away again.

"Thank you, Griff. Really. I appreciate all this, I swear I do."

I sure hope so. Because this journey may be nothing more than an irritation to Luna Lindgren, but I have a sneaking suspicion that it will ruin me for life.

Luna

"H-how are you not c-cold?"

Griff frowns at me from across the cab, his seat tilted back and his arms folded over his chest. The moonlight spilling through the windshield tints the shadows on his face deep blue, and his beard shifts as his jaw clenches.

I don't blame him for being annoyed. After all my high and mighty *I don't need a feather bed* crap, here I am hogging every single blanket from Griff's stash, and I'm still going numb from the cold. Meanwhile, Griff is sitting there in nothing but a flannel shirt, listening to my teeth chatter.

"Wait here."

The slam of his truck door echoes in the night, and I peer out into the shadows, breath held. God, even my eyeballs feel like they're freezing over, but I can't blink. Because if that wolf from earlier finds Griff alone out there, slowed down and weakened by my stealing all the blankets, if he gets hurt because of me...

The driver's door wrenches open again and I gust out a shaky sigh.

"Griff! Y-you're okay."

Even in the gloom, I see the look he gives me. Like maybe I'm going loopy as well as freezing over. "Yeah. I'm fine."

The truck dips under his weight as he climbs back inside, tugging the door shut with a final gust of freezing mountain air. "I'm out of blankets, but I keep spare clothes back there," he says, then drops a pile into his lap and holds up a balled pair of thick socks. "Give me your feet."

Hell freaking yeah. I'm not too proud to wear this man's socks. Pretending to be fine and waving off his help ended hours ago, back when my body remembered what sunshine and warm baths felt like. Now, in the depths of night, the cold is burrowing icy needles into my bones, and I'll do anything to feel better. Anything.

"M-maybe you're right. I'm not suited to mountain life."

Wriggling one stiff leg up, turning and propping my ankle boot on Griff's thighs, I wait for his crow of triumph. For him to say *I told you so* and list all the reasons I'm an idiot for coming here, of which there are many.

Instead, Griff tugs down the zipper on my ankle boot. His fingers are steady, not shaking from the cold, even though I've stolen every warm layer in his truck. "You'd get used to it. You'd dress warmer, too. Doesn't mean anything, Luna."

I gape at the world's biggest grump as he eases my boot off so gently. I only know he's doing it because I'm watching with my own two eyes, and because his big, warm hand wraps around my ankle and holds me as he tugs. My foot, meanwhile, is numb.

"Can you get frostbite out here?"

Griff's scowl deepens. He pulls a thick, woolen sock over

my ice block of a foot, then chafes me between his palms.

I watch, fascinated. I'm not even scared anymore, not with Griff taking care of business. I'm just...

Okay, this doesn't make me look good. And I'm not engineering this situation, I swear. If I had a magic wand, I would *definitely* wish I was warm again, and that we were safe in Griff's cabin for the night.

Or, um, Aiden's cabin. Whatever.

Inside, safe and cozy. That's all.

But since I *don't* have a magic wand, and we're stuck here with each other and the moonlight and my chattering teeth, I have to admit, I'm kind of... enjoying myself.

Griff's a real caretaker under all that grouchiness. His hands are achingly gentle as they carefully tug another layer over my limbs—first the socks, then a red flannel shirt drawn over my arms, and a pair of men's jeans tugged up my legs. He even buttons me into everything, eyes fixed on his hands as he works, and before he sits back again, he swaddles me back up in my pile of blankets like a burrito.

"Feeling better, city girl?"

Okay, I've officially accepted that nickname. I clearly deserve it, and it beats *princess* anyhow.

"B-better," I say.

It's true, too. Even though I'm nowhere near toasty, the extra layers have chased the worst of my shivers away. I can even feel my toes again. Burrowing the tip of my nose into my blankets, I watch Griff over the top of them like an owl.

"I'm a giant pain in your ass." My words are muffled by the fabric, but I know he hears them. There's a flash of white teeth as Griff grins.

"You are," he agrees. The truck seat creaks as he settles back again, getting comfy. "Don't mind, though."

"And you promise you don't need any blankets?" God, I'd hate if he got cold after all this. What a shitty reward for being my noble knight dressed in plaid.

"I promise."

"If I wake up in the morning and you're frozen in a block of ice, I'll be so mad, mister."

There's that grin again, racing across his rugged face so fast I nearly miss it. "Noted. Guess I'd better keep warm."

Yeah. He'd better.

But how can he do that? The longer the night goes on, the more the temperature plummets. Outside the truck, the wind moans through the trees and even the branches seem to shiver.

"Griff…"

He rolls his stiff neck, eyes closed. "Yeah?"

"You're in Mountain Rescue, right?"

We chatted a lot earlier as we first bedded down to sleep. Back when we split the blankets evenly, and our shared breaths were enough to keep the truck warm, and it was too early to drop off anyways.

I learned a lot about Griff in that sleepy chat. I learned that he's thirty six and that he's lived in this area his whole life, growing up in Cloudy Lake before moving up the mountain. I learned that he fishes and carves wood and secretly wants to learn guitar one day, and that he's not sorry his cabin doesn't have internet, not at all.

I learned that he never even considered signing up for the mail order bride program. So I guess the two of us never had a chance.

Trying not to be bitter about that.

And I told him stuff too. Told him about my job as a quilter and my crappy apartment back in the city; my sister who never answers my emails, and my passionate love for spaghetti bolognese. He asked me about being a mail order bride, because of course he did, but the weird thing is I actually told him the truth.

That I'm lonely. That I've never met a single person I connected like that with in my whole life so far, but despite it all, I want a big romance.

That I believe in fate, and I figured maybe fate needed a helping hand, so I came out here.

Griff was quiet for a long time after that.

"Yeah," he says now. "I'm in Mountain Rescue."

I chew on my bottom lip before continuing. "So that whole myth about body heat… about huddling for warmth…"

"Not a myth," he grunts.

Well, that settles it.

"Right." I grab two fistfuls of blanket and start shuffling. "Are you ready, mister? Let's do this."

* * *

"Here's one thing I don't understand."

Let's face it: one of many. But I'm curled up on Griff's lap, my cheek pillowed against the hard swell of his chest, and his big arms are pinning the blankets in place, spread out over us both. It's impossible to feel anything except blissful right now.

Every breath Griff takes, my head rocks upward an inch. I love it.

"You said the locals call it Mail Order Mountain, right? But that most of the cabins don't have WiFi. So how do all these lonely mountain men even sign up?"

Griff's chin rubs against the top of my head as he answers, low voice thick with sleep. "They hike down to Cloudy Lake. Tramp back and forth for their messages."

Oh.

Oh, my heart.

I press my face against the hollow of Griff's throat and fight the urge to howl. It'd probably attract wolves, and besides, Griff doesn't like me talking about other men—especially Aiden McRae.

He didn't tell me that. I noticed it for myself.

Though honestly, I've barely thought about my mail order fiance since meeting Griff. Doesn't that make me the biggest jerk in the world? True, I've never even met Aiden, have never done more than exchange emails, but I still came all this way for him. And he's expecting me. It'd be awful if I canceled.

But...

Could I cancel? Surely, right? And if I did...?

"Quit wriggling," Griff mumbles, but he's teasing me—I can tell. His mouth has curved up slightly beneath his beard, and he cracks one eye open to watch my reaction.

I poke my tongue out.

Griff laughs, and I'm tossed around on his rumbling, deliciously warm chest. I fit so perfectly here, and I'm not cold at all anymore, not with our bodies pressed together, and there's a gooey, molten feeling swirling low in my belly.

I keep thinking crazy thoughts. Things like *kiss him* or *rub against his thigh,* and it's only my brain's stern reminder of Aiden McRae that keeps me from doing those things.

I sure think 'em, though. God. Griff is a one-man thrill ride.

Out in the darkness, an owl hoots.

This is the best night of my life. The realization is swift and painful, and it bleeds the smile from my face. Griff notices too, because he settles back again, arms tightening.

"Get some sleep, honey."

That nickname is new, and it's different from princess or city girl. It makes the blood pump faster through my body, and it makes my heart flutter.

As I sigh and burrow into Griff's chest... I want to cry.

Griff

I wake up with a mouthful of blonde hair and the scent of lavender in my nose. Outside the truck, dawn washes over the mountainside, chasing the shadows from between tree trunks and mossy rocks. It's a blue sky day, a *cold* day with puffs of white cloud skidding overhead, and I curse myself for the thousandth time for ever risking Luna overnight in this weather.

Frost glints on the delicate ends of tree branches. It glitters on the rough bark of the fallen tree blocking the road.

I wasn't thinking. Even now, I can barely get my brain working around her.

It's no excuse. If someone else risked her like this, I'd kick their ass.

Part of me wonders if I did this on purpose. If I insisted on driving Luna out here, knowing full well we might get stuck, because I was just that hungry to be near her. But no—if I hadn't offered, she might have stayed overnight in my cabin. Slept in my bed, probably, while I crashed on the couch. Even the most shameful, selfish parts of me can see how that would have been better.

And maybe once she left, once she found her way to Aiden McRae, my sheets would have smelled like lavender.

"Hey." I shift beneath her softly snoring form. She's a bundle of warmth in my arms, and I'm so fucking relieved about that. When she asked me about frostbite last night, I wanted to slam my head into the steering wheel. "Hey. Wake up, honey. It's morning."

And if I sit here wide awake, holding her against my chest with no excuse...

Well. I won't ever be able to look Aiden McRae in the eye again.

"Mmph," Luna says. She shakes her head, inhaling sharply through her nose, then presses closer. Flattens herself against my body until there's not a single pocket of air between us.

Fuck.

I don't know what brings her back to earth. Maybe it's the sunlight filtering through the windshield; maybe it's the toasty warm air inside the cab. Maybe it's the panicked thud of my heart against her cheek, or the shameful stiffness in my jeans.

Luna goes still. "...Griff?"

I cough out a laugh. "You'd better hope so. Grizzlies aren't good cuddlers."

Oh, we can joke, but there's nothing that funny about peeling our limbs apart. About throwing off the blankets and sitting straight, blinking our bleary eyes as Luna shuffles back to her side of the cab.

Last night feels like a dream. Like it happened to two other people.

Do I look as rough as I feel? Fuck, I've never been a vain

man in all my life, but now I'm fighting the urge to check my face in the mirror. To cup a hand over my mouth and sniff my breath.

"There are mints in the glove box."

Maybe I'm not the only paranoid one, because Luna scrabbles for those mints like her life depends on them. She's already tossed two in her mouth, cracking them between her teeth, before she throws me the rest.

She looks cute in the morning. All owlish and rumpled.

Not just cute. Fucking perfect.

Ten minutes later, I'm sliding back into the cab with my head on straight and two bottles of water from my stash. I crack the lid of one and pass it over, trying not to notice the way our fingertips brush. "There you go—drink up. You can keep wearing those clothes until you've warmed up enough to take them off."

Her cheeks turn pink. Luna gapes at me for a long moment, then glances down at her borrowed red shirt with a jolt. "Oh, right." She shakes her head, frowning slightly. Still sleepy, I guess. "Yeah, okay."

Wait. What did she think I meant?

"Aiden's place isn't far." No time to worry about that now. "Even with retracing our steps and taking the rougher road, we should be there in an hour or so. He'll be worried," I add as an afterthought, rubbing a palm over my beard. If *I* were waiting for Luna in my cabin and she didn't turn up, if I thought she might be lost in the wilderness...

I'd go insane. I'd tear the world apart looking for her. I'd rip up towering trees by the roots, and I'd smash through cave walls with my bare hands. I'd wrestle a damn grizzly bear into a ravine.

"It's fine." Luna plucks at the hem of my red shirt, not looking at me. "I didn't give an exact date of arrival. Just this week sometime. It was tricky, trying to plan with the buses and the mountain, and I thought it would be romantic..."

She trails off.

I wait three heartbeats, then start the engine. The truck rumbles to life, and for the first time on this drive, I'm cold inside. So cold.

"Well, not long now." Can't think what else to say, so I clam up and start backing up the rocky path. We dip and lurch; the tires spin and I wrench the wheel. Trees watch from either side of the road, and I stare behind us until my eyes go dry.

Not long until she's with the man she wants to marry.

Then I guess it's goodbye.

* * *

I haven't spent a ton of time mulling over my bachelorhood. Unlike these others with their mail order brides and their bright, rosy hopes, I've never given it much thought.

Figured I was happy enough, thank you.

Had plenty of purpose.

And it was true—before I met Luna Lindgren. Now I'm cooked. I've had a peek behind the curtain. I've seen what could have been, have sensed what all the fuss is about, and for the first time in years as I drive the last stretch of road to Aiden McRae's cabin... I'm lonely. There's a vise wrapped around my rib cage, squeezing me tight.

Will I ever get to see her? Maybe it won't be so bad if I bump into Luna now and then. Not to try anything—god knows I'd never sniff after a married woman—but just to get a glimpse of her. Like an inoculation against all the bad stuff in the world.

A single peek once a month at her glacial eyes and her pink cheeks. The upturned tip of her nose. Her pale blonde hair, dancing on the wind...

"Will you wait for a few minutes when we get there?"

I frown at Luna, confused. Is she worried about feeling safe with Aiden? "If you want me to."

"I do." Her lips keep worrying at each other, pressing into a firm line and twisting. "I need to talk to Aiden, but... please stay."

"...Okay." I'd rather gouge out my own eyes than play third fiddle to Luna and her fiance, but alright. She's asked something of me, so I'll deliver. "You don't need to be nervous, though. Aiden is a good man. He'll take care of you."

Luna says nothing, but she scowls out of her window like we're back to insulting each other.

"Might not want to turn up dressed in my clothes, though."

Another grand huff, then she's wriggling in the passenger seat, working them off. I watch her out of the corner of my eye, eager to see her purple dress and navy leggings again.

"Thank you," Luna says, folding them sloppily and dropping the pile on the dash. I grin at her efforts. It's the most begrudging thanks I've ever received.

"Not a morning person, huh, city girl?"

The balled pair of socks sail through the cab and bounce off my temple. I laugh loud enough to drown out the engine.

* * *

Aiden McRae built his cabin against a sheer rock face. It's sheltered from the wind, tucked between pine trees on both sides, and I try to focus on that fact—that Luna will be warmer here than pretty much anywhere else, including my own cabin—to keep me from going insane.

Stones crackle beneath the tires as we pull up nice and close. No half mile hike from the road to get to Aiden's place; he's not an antisocial asshole like me. He cleared a makeshift driveway all the way up to his deck.

Did he do that for Luna? For his future wife?

She's still sitting in the passenger seat, gnawing on her bottom lip. Those blue eyes are wide, staring up at the cabin before us, and her pulse flutters below her jaw.

"Nothing to be scared of," I remind her. Fuck, why am I coaching Luna out of the truck? I should throw this piece of junk in reverse and get out of here. Should drive at breakneck pace all the way back to my cabin, and then... and then...

Then what? Can't go back in time and force her to pick *me*, can I?

It's out of my hands, anyway. The cabin door swings open, and Aiden McRae steps out, wiping his hands on a striped dishcloth.

He peers into the truck, visibly eager.

I scowl up at him, trying to find fault, any fault, in what I see. But the hard fucking fact is that Aiden McRae is probably *exactly* what all those city girls picture when they daydream about their mountain man fling. He's broad shouldered and strong, copper haired with a thick beard, and he's taciturn. Doesn't waste words when a jerk of his chin will do.

Of course, that might be down to the accident when he was a young man—the one that screwed his vocal chords.

Yeah, Aiden's not much of a talker. Guess I can see why he'd rather date via email.

"Um." Luna's still frozen beside me, plucking at her seat belt but not making any move to undo it. Aiden watches her from the deck, patient and curious, and we're like three wild animals caught in a standoff.

"I can drive away right now." Let's face it, I'm half offering for selfish reasons, but I mean it, too. Luna Lindgren will never do a single thing against her will, not while I'm around.

But: "No." She sighs and clips her seat belt undone. "I need to talk to him."

Right. She needs to meet her future husband. And apparently I need to sit here and watch it all like a third wheel.

"I'm going for a walk." The words blurt out of me before I can even think them, then I'm shoving my way out into the morning air. "Give you two some privacy. Back in ten."

"But—"

"I'll stay in calling distance. Yell if you need me, okay?"

"Griff—"

"I'll be close, I promise. Go talk to him, Luna."

My boots crunch and slide over the rock-studded dirt, and I suck in desperate mouthfuls of pine scented air as I stride between the trees. Anything to chase away the lavender. Anything to soothe my racing heart.

This is the worst fucking day of my life.

Luna

My legs are wobbly when I hop down from the truck, and I'm not sure whether that's from sleeping the night folded upright, or from pure nerves. Feels like there are hot snakes writhing in my belly. I hate stuff like this.

Well, okay, I've never been in this *exact* situation before. But I've always hated disappointing people.

"Um." My voice is hoarse, barely reaching the deck, but Aiden watches me closely. Moss green eyes catalog every detail about me, from my mussed hair and blushing cheeks to the way my fingers keep smoothing down my dress—then glance over my shoulder at where Griff strode away between the trees.

Aiden McRae raises an eyebrow.

"Hi. I'm Luna. We've, um, been corresponding…?"

Nice one, Luna. So smooth. Real cute way to talk about promising to marry someone.

Aiden nods and walks slowly down the cabin steps, his hands

tucked loosely in his pockets. Even though it's barely dawn, he looks as sharp as if he's been up for hours. There's a splash of yellow paint on the corner of his gray shirt.

He doesn't invite me inside or try to touch me. He knows already, doesn't he? He *knows*.

That makes this easier, and so much worse. Because if Aiden McRae can take one look at me and see how far gone I am for Griff, the other man must sense it too, right? And he still brought me here. He hasn't said anything.

"It's okay." The tortured sound of Aiden's voice makes me jerk, and I smooth away my surprise as fast as I can. It's like there are broken rocks in his throat, scraping together, and it sounds *painful*. "You don't have to explain. I can see you've changed your mind."

There's something resigned to this man. Like he's been holding onto a last shred of hope, fighting off a wave of bitterness, and now... now it might just engulf him.

Well, I'm the worst.

"I'm so sorry," I rush to say. "I meant my promise, I swear I did, and I was on my way here, but then I met someone and..."

Yeah. Pretty obvious who that *someone* is.

"Nothing happened," I finish lamely. "And maybe nothing will, but I have to at least try. I hope you can understand. I keep thinking that it must be... must be fate."

Aiden McRae, the man who offered me a new life in the mountains, nods slowly. He strokes one hand over his copper-flecked beard.

"Fate," he murmurs. "Sounds nice."

"Yeah." I force a nervous smile, because this is the most awkward conversation of my life, and believe me, I've found myself in some stinkers. We're saved by the crunch of Griff's boots coming back through the trees, and I smile wider, trying to hide my relief. "Okay. Well. It was good to meet you, Aiden. Sorry again."

Another nod. Another stroke of his beard, then Aiden watches Griff approach with a thoughtful expression.

"Alright." Griff won't look at me when he reaches the truck. He tugs the driver's side door open, a shower of fallen pine needles sliding off the roof onto the hard dirt below. "I'll leave you two lovebirds to get acquainted."

My stomach drops. He really doesn't care? I just threw all my plans out the window for him, and he wants me to get *acquainted* with another man?

"We changed our minds," Aiden says quietly, his low, rough voice cutting through the morning air. And though he's basically a stranger, I could kiss him for not ratting me out and telling Griff everything. He's watching me now with those knowing green eyes, and there's a glint of something there. Something like pity. Ugh. "Will you drive Luna back? Or should I take her down to town?"

Griff glances at my suitcase and sewing machine already ratchet strapped in his truck bed, as though *that's* the deciding factor. God, I hate this so much. Do they have to be so freaking practical about everything? Makes me want to pull out my own hair.

"I'll take her," Griff says at last. I press my lips in a firm line, my insides crashing together. I'm having some kind of internal earthquake, and this jerk is chatting like we're talking about the weather. "Save you the trip."

Bleurgh.

"Thanks." Aiden's already climbing the steps to his cabin, not looking back at either of us. Can't blame him. "Safe travels.

And Luna?" He pauses on the deck, one hand on the rail as he glances over his shoulder. "Maybe see you around."

Griff's attention zooms in on me again, fast as lightning. Whatever. I stomp round to the truck door and yank it open. Hey, if there's nothing between us, if he *might as well* drive me down to Cloudy Lake to save the other man a trip, then there is zero chance of me explaining Aiden's comment. He can grow old wondering about it.

Or, you know, forget it within twenty minutes of dropping me off at the bus station. Seems more likely.

* * *

"What did he mean back there?"

Griff's hands are tight on the wheel. We're bouncing back along the rocky path, seat belts snapping and straining to hold us in place, and it's a golden morning out there now. Sunshine filters through the branches, and the sky is vivid blue.

I shrug. "Dunno."

"Luna." Griff sounds ready to toss me out the window, his exasperation thick in his deep voice. Well, I'm not his biggest fan either right now. "What did Aiden mean when he said he might see you around? Are you staying in Cloudy Lake? Are you two going to… date?"

He says that last word like it tastes sour on his tongue.

"Nope."

A short huff. "Then what—"

"It doesn't matter now."

Griff curses under his breath, but he stops asking questions. We drive in silence for a long while, and I stare out of the window at two hawks wheeling high above the treeline.

Anything rather than the man sat beside me.

I thought we had something here. God, I was so *sure.* It seemed impossible that I could be the only one whose heart trips faster every time our eyes meet; the only one holding on to the truck seat by my fingernails to keep from leaping into his arms. The only one who had some kind of cosmic awakening while wrapped together last night.

My dumb, romantic heart has a lot to answer for. Of course Griff doesn't see me like that—why would he? He told me how he feels about city girls who drag their naive butts into the mountains.

At least he hasn't said 'I told you so', not even after I changed my mind. There's that, anyway.

"Bet you can't wait to see the back of me." I try to sound teasing, but it comes out strained. "What would you normally be doing at this time? If you weren't driving a city girl all over the mountain?"

Griff frowns out at the road, but he answers my question. "If I had a shift, I'd be in the Mountain Rescue headquarters down at Cloudy Lake. Or on a day off, I might be fishing at the river."

Sounds nice. I can picture it so easily: Griff, with his dark hair and scowling eyebrows and his broad, sculpted shoulders, rescuing trapped tourists who've wandered off the trail. Griff, with that secret smile he gets sometimes when he stares out at the mountains uninterrupted, casting a line into a slow-moving river. So peaceful and manly. Even in my mind's eye, I want to lick him all over.

I pretend to fix my hair so I can wipe my eyes at the same time. But I guess I'm not that sneaky, because Griff says, "*Luna.*"

Just that. Just my name. But the way he says it… he sounds

as wrecked by this morning as I feel.

"I'm fine." I sniff loudly, peering out at the mossy rocks like my life depends on it. "But it's all such a mess, you know?"

There's so much to figure out now. Need to catch up on quilting orders; need to find a new apartment. Need to decide where to go and where to live. Ugh.

Decisions are the worst.

"Aiden's an idiot." Griff's harsh words make me jolt, and I blink at the towering man beside me strangling the wheel. "If he thinks there's someone better out there, he's a fucking idiot. You're *everything*, you hear? They should put you on the goddamn mail order bride website. They should make posters with your face on and interview you on the radio. They'd have so many sign ups, their website would crash."

My watery giggle softens him up. Griff smiles at me, eyes strained.

"*You'd* never sign up."

There's a bark of laughter. "Luna, I'd be first in line."

Huh. I straighten, heart fluttering.

Ooookay. He's probably just being nice, that's all.

"Aiden didn't change his mind." Better to come clean about that, because I don't want to leave bad feelings on this mountain once I'm gone. Before long, I'll just be a distant memory to these men, and I don't want to be the reason for any bitterness between neighbors. "*I* did. But he was super nice about it. I don't think he felt any spark for me either."

"Bullshit," Griff says immediately, and it's a lie but a sweet one. "You changed your mind?"

"Yeah." I pluck at my dress, teasing at a loose thread. "Typical city girl, right?"

"Why?" Griff asks, voice hoarse.

Um. "Because we all come here unprepared, like you said, and change our minds when we figure out that it's cold as balls—"

"No," he interrupts, and the truck is slowing. Pulling onto the side of the dirt track. "Why'd you change your mind?"

Oh. Shoot.

My seat belt jerks against my shoulder as I crane to stare out of the window. "Hey, are those two hawks fighting or getting it on?"

"Luna."

"We don't get birds like that in the city." I can't look at him. I won't. I stare up at the blue, blue sky instead, chattering around the heart lodged in my throat. The trees are so huge out here, they must tickle the clouds. "Though one time, I saw this, like, pigeon orgy on my neighbor's fire escape. There were six of them, and they must have put their pigeon keys in a tiny bowl or something, because—"

"Luna," Griff says again. "Honey."

It's the *honey* that does it. I clam up, sealing my lips together tight. Tears brim in my eyes, and I'm rigid with tension as Griff reaches over and gently, oh so gently, unclips my seat belt.

"I'm not gonna push you." The strap whirs as it frees up my body. His voice is deeper than I've ever heard it. Deep and rough, filled with undercurrents of emotion. "But I really want you back in my lap for this. You gonna shuffle over?"

Gah.

I *knew* I should've taken more than one single yoga class in my entire life. The most crucial moment of my existence, and now I can't get my limbs to coordinate.

"Okay, I'm—*oof.*" Clumsy as shit, I bounce one shoulder off the dashboard then tumble into Griff's side. He plucks me up like I weigh nothing, settling my ass down on his thighs and wrapping his arms around my waist.

Heaven. This is my heaven, surrounded by his heat and his hard muscles and the kind, reverent look in his eyes.

I clear my throat, playing with his shirt collar. Flipping the corner of it back and forth over my thumb.

"Wait." Griff fumbles down the side of his seat, then shoves it back a few inches. I wriggle on his suddenly roomy lap. "Better. Okay, we got muddled for a while there this morning, but I'm thinking we're on the same page now. Am I right?"

God, I hope so. There's a swarm of butterflies crashing around in my belly. And I didn't uproot my whole life and move out to the mountains to be a weenie, so I gather the final shreds of my courage. He's set the ball rolling for us. I can do this.

Biting my lip, I walk two fingers up the line of buttons on Griff's shirt. "That depends. Are you still taking me to the Cloudy Lake bus station?"

He wheezes out a laugh. "Fuck that."

Griff's kiss is hard and hot and possessive. It's freaking *primal.* I wind my arms around his neck and sink into it, finally warm to the tips of my toes.

Griff

I'm kissing her. I'm *kissing her.* Luna Lindgren is in my lap, her plump mouth smiling against mine, and I can feel her hot breath against my cheeks.

Jesus Christ.

I rock up against her ass, clutching her closer to my chest. Can't help it. I want her closer, rougher, *more.*

"I've changed my mind about the mail order bride program." Every breath is laced with lavender. My new favorite smell. Would it grow if I planted it by the cabin? "Great invention."

Slender fingers twist in my hair and yank. "If you sign up after this, I'll smother you in your sleep with a pillow."

My laugh is muffled against her lips. "Oh, you'll be in my bed, huh?"

"Yep. Etching my name into the headboard."

I snort and palm her ass.

God, she's perfect. Every inch of her was made to fit my hands—or maybe I was made to grip her. Either way works for me.

"Luna." She's wriggling closer, settling her butt over the hard length of my cock pressing against my jeans, and I choke back a groan. "Honey, we don't have to do this right now. We can go slower."

"Maybe *you* can," she grumbles, grinding down against my length, and I huff and run my hands up to her tits. They're perfect, like her. Small and pert and soft, with two hard beads digging into the fabric of her dress. When I rub them with my thumbs, she lets out a shaky sigh.

"You ever done this before, baby?"

"Nope." My heart thunders louder in my chest, because she's giving me so much. So much trust. "But if those pigeons could figure it out…"

"I don't know." I pinch her left nipple, and her whimper sends a bolt of heat to my cock. "Those sounded like some elite level moves."

"Yeah." Luna's head tips back, her eyes heavy lidded. "Yeah, you're right. Bunch of show-offs." And now we're just talking shit to each other, barely paying attention to our words, too busy grasping and rocking; kissing and nibbling. Fuck, I could eat her in three bites.

It's everything I've been dying to do since I met her yesterday. Everything I've been craving in the depths of my soul.

"You're coming home with me after this. Back to my cabin."

Luna's mouth curves. "Yeah, I am."

"Then you're going to marry me."

She blinks, her pale eyes so close. "I am?"

I nod, trying not to act like a man suddenly finding himself on shaky ground. She's as far gone as I am, right? I'm not making a prick of myself? "Yeah, you are. So long as you want to, obviously. I mean, you came here to marry a mountain man, right? And there's one right here offering, one that you like enough to kiss, so—"

Luna flings herself against my chest, her arms so tight around my neck I can hardly breathe. Don't care. Who needs air?

"Oh, I like you plenty more than kissing, mister." Teeth graze my earlobe, and I crush her closer. So lucky. How did I get so lucky? "Maybe I should show you."

Before I register what's happening, Luna's sitting back and slender fingers tug at my belt. I blink down at them in a daze. "I've never done this before either," she says casually, like she's not short-circuiting my brain, "but I get the impression that it's beginner friendly."

Uh.

I flatten my hand over hers, pinning her fingers in place. "We're not—that's not gonna be the first thing we do, Luna."

She harrumphs, and then we're staring at each other with matching scowls. "Why not?"

Because I want to *keep* her, damn it. I want her spoiled and cherished; want her ruined for all other men. Want her to know after this, all the way down to the marrow of her bones, that she's *it* for me. A blow job ain't the way.

"Climb off for a second."

From her loud complaints, you'd think I was the worst villain in the world—but she shuffles to one side, flopping down onto the passenger seat. I shove my truck door open, and the flood of cold, pine-fresh air against my hot cheeks has never been more welcome. I shake my head as I round the truck.

Need to think straight. Need to do this right.

Luna's arms are folded when I tug her door open. I stifle a smile. "Spin around, okay? Let your legs dangle out of the truck."

"*So* bossy."

She does it, though. And when I step closer, nudging between her knees, her arms wrap around my neck in welcome.

I missed her. In the ten steps it took to round the truck, I *missed* her.

I am so far gone.

"I want to show you something," I say as she trails kisses down my neck, each press of her lips sending sparks across my skin. She nods, silvery hair tickling where it's already creeping down my collar.

"Is this a mountain man thing? Are you gonna show me how to chop wood and track an elk?"

"No." My hands spread over her thighs, gripping tight. Letting an ounce of the possessiveness I feel bleed through. "I'm going to show you what I've wanted to do to you since the first second I saw you on my deck. The very first second."

Luna gasps as I spread her legs wider. "But I... you... you *hated* me."

Oh, really?

My palms slide up her thighs, nice and slow. Mapping her, *feeling* her, until my knuckles dip under the rumpled hem of her dress and my thumbs meet on the seam of her leggings, pressing against her there.

She's hot. Hot and damp and needy, her readiness obvious even through the fabric.

"I never hated you, Luna." How could she ever think that? "I wanted you so badly it pissed me off."

"Oh," she says, her expression fragile, and then I'm kneeling on the cold, hard ground. Gonna chase every last ounce of uncertainty from her eyes. Gonna make sure Luna *knows*.

Her boots drop down to the dirt, one by one. She lifts her

hips to help me pull those leggings down, and I work them carefully over her feet, leaving her double pair of socks behind. Don't want her getting cold toes.

"Panties, too."

Luna swallows, but wriggles against the seat, then I'm tugging down a scrap of white cotton.

I pocket them. She laughs.

"Pervert. What if a bear sneaks up on us?"

My palms trail up the insides of her thighs, goosebumps rippling in their wake. Her skin is pale and creamy, dotted with freckles, and I can't wait to learn her whole body by heart. "Then I guess we're breakfast."

"And what if someone drives past on the road?"

"Then they'll get an eyeful."

Luna grins as she weaves her fingers through my hair. "Some Mountain Rescue you are."

I lean close and speak my last words against her wet heat. "I'll give you the phone number later to report me."

* * *

If I'm ever asked to name my last meal, this will be my answer. Forget fancy banquets and famous dishes, I want to eat Luna out every damn day of my life.

"This is—*ah*—are you sure it's okay?"

Her legs are draped over my shoulders, ankles locked behind my back. I've never been happier to find myself in a stranglehold.

My mouth is busy, so I answer with a growl, then do it again when the vibrations make her whimper.

She's perfect. Slick and warm and salty-sweet. Opening for

me, spreading wide with so much trust, and I just want to rub my whole fucking face on her.

Luna hisses out a laugh, bucking against my chin. "Your beard tickles."

Sliding a palm under her ass, I knead her flesh as I suck on her clit. Then grip her tighter, tilting her up for me as I slide my tongue deep inside her channel.

"Oh, you're—*Griff.*"

She's tugging on my hair harder now. Wriggling and writhing on the passenger seat of my truck, the leather creaking beneath her bare ass. My knees are going numb on the frosty ground, and the wind's whistling against the back of my neck, but I don't care.

This is heaven.

Can't believe I nearly lost her. Can't believe I nearly drove her to the goddamn bus station and waved her off like an idiot, letting her go away from me forever when we could've had *this.*

My heart is raw. I can't even handle the thought of it.

"Luna," I mumble against her slick flesh. "Fuck, Luna. You're mine, you hear?"

She shivers and laughs, the sound cutting off with a gasp. Then I'm lapping at her clit and pumping a finger inside her, rubbing at her walls as I try to get her off—

Yes.

As her body clamps down on my fingers, as her eyes go wide and her cheeks burn bright pink, victory has never felt so sweet.

And thank fucking god. I *need* to get inside her.

Pins and needles shoot through my legs as I lumber to my feet. All grace has gone, and I'm not smooth at all as I yank my belt open, but Luna doesn't seem to mind. She plucks at my sleeve and whispers about hurrying up; she shuffles her ass forward on the seat, spreading her thighs even wider, ready for me.

"Might hurt a bit the first time." Really hope not. I want this so badly my lungs hurt. "I'll go slow, okay? And if you want me to stop at any point, just say the word—"

"Griff." Luna wraps a cool hand around my cock and it jerks against her palm. A hiss escapes between my teeth as she guides me to her entrance. "Stop fussing. I want this."

Arms around my shoulders; lavender-scented hair blowing against my cheeks. Heat and wetness and a strangling vise grip on my cock—it's all a messy, perfect blur.

Luna whimpers and I freeze, my length buried halfway inside her, but then her heels dig into my ass. "Keep going! That was a happy sound."

"Yeah?" My heartbeat slams in my ears, and I press our foreheads together. Rock my head from side to side as I press deeper, *deeper,* so far inside my girl that I can feel her pulse too, tripping along faster than mine. "It feels good?"

"*So* good," she gasps.

Well, then.

I grit my teeth and focus on breathing slowly, in and out. In and out. For the next few minutes, I hold myself in check, and I squeeze Luna's ass, and I thrust steadily until I'm all the way in, as close as I can possibly get.

"Jesus." Sweat prickles down my spine. There's a ringing sound in my ears. "You feeling this, Luna?"

"Uh-huh." Her hands tremble as they grip two fistfuls of my shirt. Her mouth tugs up at one corner, and she's staring up at me with so much love, it floors me. "Kind of hard to miss."

Yeah, no kidding. My life will forever be split into two eras: before this moment, and afterward. Before Luna (BL) and Sweet Fucking Heaven (SWF).

"You sure you want to keep going?"

Her scoff is music to my ears. Then her ankles hook together behind my back, and she yanks hard on my shirt.

"Oh, I'm sure. Give me everything you've got."

Luna

It's easy to talk a big game, isn't it? Easy to spout nonsense, eager to impress the heartbreaker of a mountain man currently buried between your thighs, but when he grins down at you with a feral glint in his eyes, that confidence is harder to keep around.

"Careful what you wish for, Luna." He's already moving, rocking against me. Shallow thrusts at first, letting me get used to his thick length sawing in and out, then moving harder. Slamming between my legs.

And for a second, the worry creeps in. The paranoia of whether I'm doing this right, whether I'll measure up, whether my instincts are enough to carry me through.

Then Griff lets out a low groan, his chest heaving as he pounds into me, and he looks at me with so much raw desire that every doubt evaporates like morning mist.

And I must be insane, because I lean back with a wild laugh, feeling the mountain wind in my hair, and I lift my hips. Meet him thrust for thrust. I can do this. It's easy, when I let it be.

It's *right*.

And it feels so freaking good that my eyes could cross.

"Jesus," Griff says again, his voice hoarse. He keeps squeezing my ass, my thighs, my hips; he pinches my nipples and licks my throat. "Fuck, Luna. This is—I could do this forever."

"We will," I promise him. "The rest of our lives."

And though that declaration would scare off ninety nine percent of men, Griff gusts out a breath and fucks me harder, *slower*, digging inside me like he could plant himself there. Like he wants to leave his imprint everywhere, even on the inside of my body.

"I'll build you a nicer deck. Your own cabin too, if you want one. However the fuck that quilting machine works, I'll build you a special cabin to use it in, and I'll use the best trees for it. The whole thing will smell like heaven."

I think this is the mountain man version of writing me a poem. Woodwork and forest skills.

"Can't wait." I suck a bruise on Griff's throat, just below his beard. His skin is salty from sweat, and he's breathing hard from rocking into me, fighting to get closer, practically chasing me back into the truck. "I can't build you anything, but that blow job's still on the table. Unless you want a quilt?"

His laugh vibrates through my whole body, and my toes curl behind his back.

Somewhere further down the mountain, a truck engine roars behind the trees, and we should stop this, should get out of sight, should think straight, but we can't. We can't. We can't.

It's too good.

Too urgent.

And when Griff squeezes my thighs hard enough to bruise, I hiss with pleasure; when I bite down on his shoulder, he makes a rough noise in the back of this throat. We're lost to each other, feverish and wild, and it's sticky and primal and perfect.

"You're *mine*," he says again, breath misting hot against my cheek.

"Uh-huh." I yank harder on his shirt. "Then *show me.*"

In the end, it happens so naturally. Crests over me like a wave. One minute I'm clinging on to Griff's shirt, whispering filthy nothings against his throat, feeling the thick, wet slide of his cock between my legs. The next, he slides a hand between us, his thumb finding my clit, and then...

Heat roars through every inch of my body. It's a wildfire, ravenous and searing, and I'm left shuddering and gasping for breath, twitching and moaning in Griff's eager hold. He lets out a savage sigh of triumph, kissing me so hard my head tips back, and then one, two, three thrusts later, he stills inside me.

Twitches and swells.

And spills wet heat deep in my core.

It's so delicious, I nearly tip over the edge again, letting out a strangled groan and pressing my forehead into his shoulder. It feels so *right.* The jagged pieces inside me finally slot into place.

Ten minutes and one unlucky spare shirt wiped between my legs later, Griff tucks a lock of hair behind my ear. "Ready to go home, Luna?"

Like you wouldn't believe.

* * *

Three years later

"Okay, cast your line. Watch your hook, just like I showed you. Nice and easy and—yeah. Just like that."

Griff's a good teacher. I hide a smile as I peer out at the river, ripples spreading from where my line just dropped.

"Alright. Now what?"

"Now we wait." He sounds amused. Damn him. "Or are you in some kind of hurry, city girl?"

Whatever. I poke my tongue out at my husband, grinning when he laughs, then sink back into one of the chairs he set out for us on the river's edge. It's a quiet spring day, the breeze cool and floral, and the mountains are waking from their deep winter sleep.

"When you go out fishing for hours, I always picture you working harder than this, you know? Wrestling giant salmon into submission. Maybe hunting with one of those long spears."

Griff smiles faintly as he notches my rod into a special stand, leaning it upright so I don't need to hold on. "Sorry to disappoint."

"I bet chopping wood is easy too."

"Probably."

"And Mountain Rescue."

"Anyone could do it."

"Thought so."

I sigh happily, plucking at my green dress where it rests over my baby bump. Not long now, and then our cabin will be a lot less restful. Messier, too.

Don't care. I'm so, so excited. Every time I feel a little kick inside my belly, I practically float up to the rafters with love. Will the baby like fishing?

"Quilting, on the other hand." Griff frowns out at the treeline, aggrieved, as he settles into his own chair. "That was… harder than I expected."

Ha. He has *no* idea. I gave him the easiest possible thing to make, and he still went through some kind of fabric-based trauma. Kept cursing under his breath and stabbing himself in the thumb with a needle, bitching about how it was all so fiddly.

Each to their own. And it works for us—this division of skills. We match each other perfectly, filling in each other's gaps.

"But how long until the fish come?"

Griff's eyes crinkle as he smiles. "As long as it takes." He nods at my belly. "Come on, Luna. You know the best things take time."

So they do. I feel like I waited for *him* for a whole lifetime.

Still. I stroke my bump and watch ripples spread across the river surface.

Not much longer now.

II

Lonely Beard

Description

I came to this mountain for market research.

Now I'm sheltering from a storm with a bearded grump.

Aiden McCrae has an attitude problem. Hey, maybe *that's* why he can't keep a mail order bride—but when I lose my cool and suggest that to him, waving my clipboard on his deck, he sends me away without another word.

I don't get far, though. Not when my car won't start as a storm lashes against the mountainside. It's dangerous out here, and I'm about as nature-proof as my skirt suit.

Let's face it: I'm doomed. I'm gonna be struck by lightning, or eaten by a bear, or washed away by this torrential rain.

But insult or not, Aiden lets me shelter in his cabin... and my research has just begun.

Grace

⁂

"Name?"

"Aiden McRae."

"Age?"

"Thirty four."

I scribble the answers on my clipboard, the paper of my survey rustling in the wind, and feel the back of my neck blush under this man's gaze. He watches me from the front door of his cabin, arms folded over his broad chest, and his green eyes are hard with impatience.

What's the rush? Is there some wood-choppin' that just can't wait? Does he have a strict appointment with a whittling knife?

I blow out a short breath.

Professionalism. Yes.

All around us, pine trees stab toward the clouds, branches shivering in the frosty wind. The dark sky churns above the mountains, and boy, I'd better get a move on. Don't want to drive my tiny rental car back down the mountainside in bad weather.

"Thank you for taking the time to speak to me today, Mr McRae." Especially with that voice of his. Deep and gruff and broken. When this man speaks it sounds like there's a landslide of jagged rocks in his throat, and I fought a wince the first time I heard it. "We at Soulmate Express are determined that all of our clients will find love through the mail order program. Whatever has been going wrong, I assure you we can fix it."

Let's hope so, anyway. Because this man has scared off three mail order brides in the last eight months, and those odds are not in our favor. We vet all of our clients extensively, but if the problem is *him*...

Well. That's what I'm here to figure out.

Low words scrape from his throat. "I already left the program."

My clipboard lowers an inch. "You... what?"

No one leaves Soulmate Express. Not until they're blissfully happy. It's the whole freaking point of the company, the whole reason I don't mind working myself into a ragged heap for my job. I—*we*—change people's lives.

And I have a perfect record with my clients. Aiden McRae is not leaving us without a soulmate on his arm.

His toned, flannel-shirt-wearing arm.

Okay, come on. I drop my clipboard and stare at the man in front of me, appraising him openly for the first time since I arrived. With his coppery hair and short beard, his sculpted body and scarred hands, he should be catnip for any woman signed up to Soulmate Express.

I mean, he's *gorgeous.* Steal-your-breath gorgeous. If we put him on the website, sign ups would leap, except we have a strict policy about exchanging photos before our clients meet. We think it's better to fall in love with someone's personality first, then let the rest follow.

Personally, I wouldn't know. I work such long hours, when would I ever date?

"You can't leave the program," I say flatly. "You haven't found love yet."

Those green eyes narrow. Aiden says nothing.

"*So,*" I push on, like he asked instead of glowering at me like that, "we have work to do, the two of us. We're going to figure out where we've been going wrong so I can make you better matches. And we'll work on your, uh..."

Aiden's eyebrow lifts.

"Demeanor."

When he finally speaks, my stomach swoops with triumph. He's engaging with the process! There's hope for us yet. For Aiden's love life, and for my perfect record. "You made my matches?"

"Yes, and—"

"No. I'm done."

I splutter, holding my clipboard up between us. The wind's getting stronger, howling over the mountainside and tugging at my skirt suit. The frosty air cuts clean through the fabric, slicing right to my bare skin beneath, and I fend off a shiver.

I will *not* look weak in front of this man. Not this jerk who keeps watching me so calmly and with such disdain, like he knows *exactly* what sort of person I am and finds me seriously lacking.

"Look, Mr McRae. I have a perfect record at Soulmate Express. Do you understand? I *always* find my clients their soulmates, and so help me, I will find yours too—"

"No."

Ugh! I smooth a hand over my bun, my fingers trembling

with frustration.

"This isn't about you." He says it slowly, like I'm a small child who keeps trying to bother the grown ups. Tugging on his pants leg while he's busy with the game. "Or your record. And I'm done."

Is he serious? I *flew* here for this conversation. I took a flight and hired a car; I drove up that crazy, snaking mountain path; I ate a drive-through burrito dangling out of the car window so I wouldn't stink up the leather, all so I could meet Aiden McRae and find his soulmate once and for all.

And you know, if he'd answered one of my dozens of emails, I wouldn't have had to come at all. But hey. Guess he's too busy scowling at trees to check his inbox.

"Mr McRae." I pour every last ounce of my professionalism into my next words, forcing my shoulders down and a polite smile onto my face. "I understand that failed matches can be a very painful experience for our clients, but I'm here to ensure that next time—"

"No." He starts to close the door. He's closing the freaking door in my face!

"Maybe it's you!" I yell without thinking, my temper finally surging up my throat, because this has been the longest day of my existence, and it's ending with a door slammed in my face. Asshole. "Maybe it's your bad attitude, Mr McRae. Maybe that's what scares your matches off."

Slowly, so slowly, the door swings open again. Past his shoulder, in the warm glow of his cabin, I catch a glimpse of a bookcase and sofa; a table and the corner of a bed.

I wrench my gaze back to his, cheeks flaming.

Aiden McRae doesn't call me out on my rudeness. He doesn't threaten to get me fired. He stares at me for a long, long time, his eyes cold and jaw hard, and all the while I strangle my clipboard between us.

Then he jerks his chin at the rental car parked behind me on the dirt path.

Guess I'm not worth words anymore. That's fair. It sounds pretty painful when he speaks.

"Think about what I said." I turn with a huff and clomp down the cabin steps, my ballet flats sliding on the damp wood. It really ruins my dramatic exit when I nearly slip on the last step, grabbing for the handrail with a squeak.

Aiden McRae is silent as ever, watching me go.

This day. This freaking *day*. And it's still only half over for me. I still need to drive back down the mountainside and return the hire car to the airport; need to wait for my flight then finally, *finally* go home.

I'm going to eat a whole tub of salted caramel ice cream before bed. Don't care about nutrients, not tonight.

Then I'm going to burrow under my covers and never think about Aiden McRae again. Asshole.

* * *

"Come on. Oh, come *on*."

I turn the key in the ignition, mentally praying to any deities that might be listening. The world can't be this cruel, right? My hire car can't have broken down ten feet from Aiden McRae's cabin. It's not possible.

"I will be a better person," I mutter under my breath. "I'll, um, I'll feed the birds at the park. And I'll floss every night before bed. I'll even do that stupid charity 5K, the one where everyone dresses up like a bumblebee—"

The car engine sputters, then falls silent.

I yank the key out, squeezing it until it jabs into my sweaty palm, and meet my own crazed eyes in the rear view mirror, brown strands of hair escaping my bun. My chest heaves with each deep breath.

"Not. Happening."

I can't break down *here*. Not where there's no phone signal; not where a man who clearly hates me can see everything. Not on a freaking mountain, with towering, snow-capped peaks high above and a moaning wind that keeps shoving the car until it rocks.

My panicked breaths are fogging the mirror. "Grace," I command myself. "Fix this."

Because at twenty three years old, I am the fixer of my own life. I pay my bills; cook all my dinners; snake my own shower drain. When I moved into my current apartment, schlepping halfway across the city, *I* moved every single box. No one else.

I'm no damsel in distress. And Aiden McRae can ruin my perfect record, but he can't render me helpless with his knowing green eyes. This is a challenge, but it's one I can solve.

…Not that Aiden's watching right now. That cabin door is sealed shut, and he's tucked away in that warm glow, safe from the wind. Can he hear my failed attempts at starting the car? Is he laughing with that deep, broken voice of his?

Seriously. How is the wind blowing *inside* this rental car? I shiver, slotting the key in the ignition again.

Three more attempts, then my forehead thunks onto the steering wheel. Drops of rain patter against the roof of the car, gently at first, then faster, harder, until a gale pounds against the metal and echoes until my ears ring.

"Bleurgh," I grumble, rocking my head from side to side. The bumpy leather of the steering wheel digs into my forehead.

One more minute of self pity. One more minute, then I'll fix this.

When I finally sit up, the mountain is transformed. The orderly lines of pine trees are bowed down, branches thrashing, needles torn away by the raging winds. It's raining so hard that the windshield is a constant waterfall, and it's getting darker by the second.

"Crap." I try the engine again, mouth dry. This isn't just the world's shittiest day, this is...

Am I going to die out here?

Lightning spears through the gloom, sparks flying from a nearby tree, and I throw my hands over my head with a whimper. Thunder rumbles all around, loud enough to shake the earth, and this is it, this is how I go, I'm going to meet my maker while wearing a charcoal skirt suit—

"Hey!" The pounding of a fist against the car window sinks into my brain. I turn and gape at a soaking wet Aiden McRae, his coppery hair and beard darkened by the rain. He waves for me to get out of the car, his movements choppy.

I'm clumsy and uncoordinated. It takes a few tries for my fingers to work, but when I get the car door open, I shove it wide against the wind and topple out onto the dirt track.

A solid chest stops my fall.

Blinking up at my savior, rain streaming into my eyes, I'm numb with terror.

Then lightning splits the air again, there's another shower of sparks and my shriek hurts my throat—as I'm yanked toward the cabin.

Aiden

⁓ ❧❧ ⁓

"**D**ry off."

I toss a folded blue towel at the girl shivering just inside my front door, the fabric of her prissy little skirt suit sticking to her limbs. Underneath the blazer, her white shirt is translucent. What did she say her name was? Grace?

With her bedraggled dark hair slipping out of its bun, her rumpled wet clothes and the bright red tip of her nose—she doesn't look especially graceful. She looks like a drowned rat in office wear.

The floorboards creak as I stride across the room to the log burner, prodding at the fire with a poker. It hisses and pops as the flames leap higher, and another wave of warmth spreads through my cabin.

Good. My own clothes are soaked, clinging to my skin, and already a chill has snaked down my spine. Don't want to think about how frozen my interloper is.

"Um."

At the sound of her voice, I screw my eyes shut and suck in a deep breath, still crouched in front of the fire. She's going to keep talking, isn't she? Going to keep asking all those questions. My chest twists, and everything feels so raw.

Shouldn't have brought her in here. Should never have answered my damn door. But then she'd still be stuck out in that storm, wouldn't she? And that's no good either.

"Um," Grace says again, her voice trembling in the quiet. "Mr McRae?"

She's not half as ballsy as she was thirty minutes ago, and the weird thing is... I miss it. There was something special about watching her rant and rave, jabbing at me with her clipboard. Like her spark was contagious, lighting me up from the inside, making me feel truly alive for the first time in months.

Now she's curled in on herself, sniffling from the cold. Dimmed.

"Stand by the fire." Fuck, my throat is ruined after calling to her through the storm. Every word slices like a blade on its way out. "Warm up. Get dry."

"Thank you," she says.

There are two soft thumps as she kicks off her ruined shoes, and then she pads barefoot across my cabin, dripping a trail of rainwater as she goes, her borrowed towel wrapped around her shoulders like a cape. She passes the coffee table I carved last spring, piled high with books from the Cloudy Lake public library, dipping her chin to scan the titles. She spots my paintings on the walls, too, her steps slowing as she goes past, and heat crawls up my neck.

Grace is the last person I want to see these parts of me. They're private, damn it, and once she knows them, they'll probably be noted down in my Soulmate Express file, another data point for her to chew over and wonder where she went wrong with my failed matches.

It's no mystery. *I'm* the one who messed up. Should never have signed up for the mail order program.

That's what happens when you let the Cloudy Lake librarian slip a bunch of romance novels into your stack of books about woodcraft. You start getting *ideas*, but real life isn't like that, is it?

"These are beautiful," Grace murmurs, pointing at the nearest painting—a vivid dream-scape of the forest done in oils. Ghostly owls surround a clearing, feathers blurring into the trees, and the stars seem to pulse off the canvas.

She's still gripping her towel, the fabric clutched between her knuckles. "Did you do them?"

Damn it. "Yeah."

For once, she seems to get that I don't want to chat. That, or she decides not to risk it while the storm's going strong outside. Grace walks to the log burner, and I try not to notice her bare toes scrunching into my rug; try not to stare at the high arches of her feet.

Look, I'm not a foot guy or anything. Okay? I don't get worked up over toes, but I'd give my right arm to paint this girl. Her bone structure is a work of art already, and those brown eyes are pure soul.

Maybe I could paint her stretched out on my sofa, tangled in a tartan blanket, or out on my deck in the golden light of summer...

Provided Grace could keep quiet, anyway. She's way too eager to discuss my non-existent love life, and who the hell wants that?

"It's a rental," she tells me, teeth chattering as she warms her back by the fire. The air smells of damp fabric and wood smoke. "The car, I mean."

"It's a piece of shit."

A bright grin chases across her face, then it's gone. A split second of that spark, teasing me. "Yeah, no kidding. But I have the number for the hire company, and as soon as the storm lets up, I'll head down to Cloudy Lake and call them. I'll fix this, Mr McRae."

I don't doubt it. This woman is a force of nature, the same as those winds outside.

We both pause, listening to the storm. It's raging out there, muffled by the thick, wooden walls of my cabin, but still deadly. There's no way she's stepping foot in that—not if I have any say.

I may be a grumpy asshole, but I won't let her get hurt on my watch. Not even with my *bad attitude.*

"You need clothes?"

If she's good and soaked, standing by the fire won't do much. Grace plucks at the fabric of her skirt, nose wrinkling at the squelching noise. "Um, maybe. Or—yes. Yes please, Mr McRae."

"Aiden." I cross to the solid wood dresser against the wall by the bed, and pull out a heavy drawer. No point standing on ceremony, not when I've seen her soaked to the skin, every dip and curve of her lean form so stark, and not when she's about to wear my clothes against her bare body. "Call me Aiden."

The storm could last a long while, after all.

Might as well get comfortable.

* * *

"Okay, so here's your first problem."

Twenty minutes later, dressed in a forest green woolen sweater and not much else, Grace marches around my cabin like a general addressing her troops. Her bare legs are long and smooth, her damp hair loose around her shoulders, and though the hem hangs nearly to her knees, my stomach keeps dipping at the sight of her.

Should have tried harder to find her a pair of shorts or something. But she insisted that it was fine, that the sweater came down lower than her skirt, and I'm enough of an idiot that I agreed.

Now I can't focus. What is she yammering about?

"My problem?"

Grace snorts and stops by the front door to my cabin, jabbing a triumphant hand at the nearest wall. My whittling knives hang on nails, arranged in a display of sharp metal. Hey, I like to whittle.

"What's the first thing your matches see when they enter the home of a man they don't know? Oh, look. The serial killer starter set, hung proudly on the wall."

I scratch my beard, frowning at the knives. "They're for whittling. Carving wood."

A flash of private amusement dances across her brown eyes, then Grace folds her arms. "You know I'm right about this, Mr McRae."

"Aiden." And okay, yeah. I could see how the knives might not help, *if* I planned on trying any more matches. But I'm done. "This doesn't matter," I remind her, but Grace strides past like I never spoke. A whiff of vanilla trails in her wake.

"These, on the other hand, are perfect." She stops in front of my paintings again, raising her arms like she's praying to the paint-splattered canvas. "Men who can paint are super sexy."

…They are? Does Grace think that, or is it supposedly common knowledge?

"Doesn't matter," I grind out again.

But even with my protests, I still trail the matchmaker around my cabin, listening to her assessment of the first impression I make. My sofa: austere. My bookcase: says I'm thoughtful. My bed: very inviting.

My gut swoops again at that last one.

"I mean it looks comfortable," she explains quickly, and thank god I'm not the only one blushing. We stand near the edge of the mattress together, determined not to meet the other's eye. "The covers look soft and recently laundered, and you actually made the bed when you got up this morning. That's good."

I rub the back of my neck. "Low bar."

Grace's chuckle throws me off balance. "You have no idea."

But I think I do, actually. I read those emails from my matches, bemoaning the lack of decent men in their real lives; I've pulled up a stool in the Cloudy Lake bar and overheard the local women's woes. I know that it's rough out there when you're looking for love.

"Maybe it's my demeanor." I mean it as a joke, but it comes out bitter. And Grace elbows me gently, her mouth curving into a smile.

"We can fix that too. Want to show me your moves?"

Oh, let me think about that.

That's right: I'd rather die.

Grace

❧ ⚬⚬⚬ ❧

"I told you." Aiden looks thunderous as I drag him by the elbow, positioning him in front of the door. "I don't have moves, Grace."

Yeah, right. "Pretend I'm on the deck and you've just answered the door. It's too cold and wet out there, but you get it. I'm your bride."

"Oh, I think I can keep up," he snaps. He's so irritated that two bright spots of color burn on his cheeks, and his broad shoulders are rigid beneath his fresh gray shirt. I keep stealing glances at his sturdy collarbone peeking from his open collar, my eyes moving of their own accord.

I don't want to be a perv, but Aiden McRae makes it very hard not to stare. Seriously, how could those idiots turn this man down? He's tall and strong and broody and capable. He paints and he smells like pine. If someone were to create my dream mountain man in a lab, well...

I shut that thought down, pronto. Aiden is a client. Or he will be again soon, anyway.

"Okay." I wave a hand at him, bouncing on my toes. "Show me what you've got."

"Grace." Aiden looks ready to walk out into the storm and toss himself down a ravine. "I never tried any fucking moves, and I'm done anyway. This is pointless."

"You must have done *something*—"

"I spoke," he bites out, green eyes narrowed on mine, daring me to mock him over this. "I spoke, and the first two matches heard my voice and turned on their heels. Is that something you can fix?"

I stop bouncing, suddenly queasy. The cabin is so warm, maybe *too* warm, the fire crackling in the burner, and I'm weirdly lightheaded. "That's why they canceled the match? Your voice?"

Aiden folds his arms over his chest and glares at me.

"We have these questionnaires," I say helplessly, like my world isn't crumbling around me, because I made those stupid matches. Soulmate Express is my whole life, and I put Aiden in that position. "We vet everyone who signs up to the program… we make sure their priorities are right…"

"Guess people are different in real life than on paper."

Crapping crapsticks. How did I go so wrong?

"And your third match?" I don't really want to ask, but I did this. I should face whatever monster I set Aiden up with last. She probably wore a puppy fur coat or tried to steal his life savings—but this time his expression softens a bit.

"Luna's sweet," he allows, tipping his chin. "She's a good neighbor. And she's a good wife to Griff."

…Neighbor? *Griff*?

"Who the hell is Griff?" Glancing down, I notice I'm wringing my hands together. I drop my arms, trying to look like a normal person. Over in the log burner, the fire spits out a flurry of sparks.

Aiden watches my discomfort with one eyebrow raised. "The man who ruined your perfect record. You want to hunt him down with a whittling knife?"

So Aiden did like Luna, then. That's... good.

My stomach doesn't ache at all.

"Okay. Well. If you tell me what you liked about Luna, I could find you someone else like her—"

"I didn't," he interrupts. "I mean, she's sweet. Like I said. But I wasn't sad about the canceled match. I didn't, you know. Feel anything."

Aiden frowns at my feet as he speaks, bundled up in a borrowed pair of red knitted socks. I scrunch my cozy toes against the floorboards, a maelstrom of different feelings crashing around inside me, rougher than the storm howling outside.

There's shame and horror—about those failed matches. *My* failures.

There's curdling jealousy over his calling this Luna girl 'sweet'.

And relief—bright, stupid relief—that he didn't really click with her anyway. What is wrong with me? I'm not signed up to Soulmate Express. This man is not an option for me.

"Grace?" He sounds so patient, moss green eyes flicking up to mine. I don't deserve this kindness. "I'm done talking about this. Alright?"

My temples throb as I nod, because I may be the fixer, but even I have to admit when I'm slamming my head against a brick wall.

"I'll cook dinner," Aiden says, briefly squeezing my shoulder before he walks away. Like I'm the one who needs comforting, even though I've done nothing but bring this man trouble.

I watch him go, feeling completely lost.

Now what do I do?

* * *

"You have electricity in your cabin. And running water."

Here's what I've learned over the last hour or so: when in doubt, pester Aiden McRae. It's a surefire hit of happiness, and I need one of those right now. I need it bad.

Sure enough, the mountain man glances at me from where he's stirring a pot of chili on the stove, his expression wry. "What a world."

"Do all the cabins on the mountain have power and water?"

"No." The wooden spoon knocks gently against the rim of the pot, chunks of sauce dropping back into the chili. It smells spicy and savory and freaking amazing. Like roasted tomatoes and sizzling beef. My stomach keeps growling louder than the thunder outside. "But it's not hard to get a generator and a water tank going."

I bet it is hard. And I bet Aiden dismisses a lot of his skills like that—as something anyone could do. Bullshit, I say.

"You should pimp your cabin out more on your Soulmate profile."

He sighs, checking the saucepan of boiling rice. "Because that's what I want my match to fall in love with. My real estate."

Fair point. I flick at a jar of wooden spoons and spatulas, chewing on my bottom lip.

"What's your place like?" Aiden asks suddenly, and it's such a surprise that I blurt out an honest answer.

73

"Lonely."

He goes quiet, stirring the chili.

"I mean, it's a cute apartment," I hurry to add. Why did I tell him that? "There's a reading nook in one window, and I always wanted one of those growing up. Though I don't have much free time to read anyway, and actually the only things I've read there have been work reports and client profiles, but I like my nook. I sewed my own cushions to decorate it."

Aiden grunts. I think that means, "Please, go on."

"I thought about getting a cat to keep me company, but it doesn't seem fair. I'm barely home, you know? Always at the office or out at networking events. Flying out to meet grumpy mountain men, et cetera. And even the grouchiest cats like to berate their owners now and then."

"So no soulmate match for you?" If Aiden stares any harder at the chili, it's gonna part like a lumpy red sea.

"Ha." My elbow digs into his ribs and he shifts an inch closer. Heat spreads over my side, and I'm reminded again how big and solid he is. How muscled and manly. Oof. "Employees don't use the service. That would be super inappropriate."

"Right."

There's another long silence, and this time, there's more simmering in this cabin than a pot of chili. Something warm and gooey; something that makes my tummy flutter. I open my mouth—then close it again. Other people's love lives, those are easy, but my own? God help me.

Doesn't matter. Inappropriate. Gah.

"Will it be much longer?" I lean over and inhale the spicy steam. When was the last time someone else cooked for me? I can't remember, but I am *excited*. "I'm starving."

* * *

Two heaping bowls of chili and one food baby later, I lay sprawled on Aiden's rug. The fire crackles in the log burner, the heat scorching one side of my face, but I'm too sleepy and full to move. His woolen sweater is so soft and comfy, and my toes are toasty in my borrowed socks. I'm a happy little dormouse.

Have I ever been this relaxed before? Doubt it. And somehow, the branches cracking and wind roaring outside only make me feel cozier.

"Okay, I get it." I wave a clumsy hand in the air, like I'm casting a spell over the whole firelit cabin. "I get the appeal. The whole mountain man thing."

"Oh yeah?" Aiden's stretched out on the rug by my side, arms folded behind his head, his customary frown pinned on the rafters. We both took one look at the austere sofa after dinner then melted onto the floor by the fire. "You gonna marry one of my neighbors too?"

I snort. "Hardly. No, I mean, I get the cabin life. Cozying up in the wilderness; chopping firewood and jumping in piles of leaves. Inviting packs of wolves around for tea and all that."

"I'm not sure you do." Aiden's broken voice sounds amused. When he turns to face me, his green eyes twinkle. "Is all your information straight from a storybook?"

"Pretty much."

His beard shifts as he grins. "Explains a lot."

We lapse back into companionable silence, and it hits me like one of those lightning bolts tearing up the mountainside: this is what I've been missing. This is the source of the dull ache in my life. I've been so freaking lonely, and I've been working too hard to even notice it.

Being here with Aiden, our steady breaths falling into sync… it's like medicine.

Aiden must be lonely too. Why else would he sign up for Soulmate Express? And yet his matches failed, and he's still here all alone, and I hate that. I hate that I let him down. And now he's given up.

"It doesn't make any sense," I huff, glaring up at the rafters. "It just—it makes no sense."

Aiden rolls onto his side, coming to face me with that frown. "What doesn't?"

I jab a hand up and down the length of his whole body. "This! You're like… okay, say we're in a nature documentary, okay? We're two monkeys. Or baboons. You and me and all the people signed up to the mail order program, say we're baboons and we're all pure instinct. Animals."

"…Okay." Aiden's watching me closely, like I might need to be wrestled into a padded room at any moment. Whatever.

"And using my pure baboon instincts, I can tell you that you're the whole primal package. You know? You're big and strong and smart and funny. You have a nice nest," I wave an arm wildly around the cabin, "and you're super capable. You can hunter-gather for future baboon babies."

"This is a weird storybook."

"No, *listen*. You're like this flawless alpha baboon. You're the king of the jungle."

"I think that's lions."

I growl and snatch a cushion off the nearby sofa, tossing it at Aiden's head. He catches it, laughing, as I yell, "It doesn't matter! My point is, you're *it*. What more could anyone possibly ask for?"

The laughter drains slowly from Aiden's face, leaving an odd smile behind. Then we're both sitting up, both flushed, both breathing hard. My hair is mussed and the sweater hem keeps sliding up my thighs. I know, because I keep catching him looking.

"Baboons?" Aiden asks at last, running a hand over his bristly jaw. "Really?"

I'm not sure which of us moves first. Not sure when the air changed in the room, going from peaceful and warm to crackling with energy, a metallic taste on my tongue. Like the thunderstorm has come inside, seeping through the cracks around the door frame, and now we're caught up in the madness.

All I know is one moment, I'm tossing cushions and yelling about baboons, and the next I'm crawling into Aiden McRae's lap, his hands gripping tight to my hips. The firelight casts a golden glow over his face, brings out the copper tint to his hair, and there's a hungry edge to him that I didn't notice before. The lines of his face are stark.

"Grace." Aiden stares down between us at where my thighs part over his lap. At the smooth, olive skin of my bare legs, and the hem of his green sweater grazing the black cotton of my panties. He can't seem to tear his eyes away from the sight of his hands on my body, his scarred artist's fingers delving into the folds of my borrowed sweater, mapping the feel of me beneath the wool. "Grace, we can stop this. Okay? I don't expect this. I won't send you out into the storm."

Duh.

He may be grumpy, but Aiden McRae is a good man. The best. So I bite my lip and flick his shirt button open. Just the top one—just enough to see the whole hollow of his throat.

Jeez Louise. This man is a walking work of art, a sculpture in a gray flannel shirt, and the drama of the storm must have addled my brains, because I lean forward and lick his collarbone.

Aiden groans, squeezing my hips tighter. "*Grace.*"

This is fine. He's not a client anymore. It's not inappropriate.

It's not the most earth-shattering experience of my life.

"I don't know what I'm doing," I admit as I sit back, breathless and flushed.

Aiden's mouth twitches. "Me neither. Good thing we're pure baboon instinct."

"Oh, you—"

Aiden bears me down onto my back on the rug, and I shut the hell up.

Aiden

The sight of Grace in that baggy green sweater has been driving me out of my mind for hours. I've been yanking my gaze away from her thighs; have been wrestling my thoughts under control through sheer force of will, but not before heated images flashed across my brain, tormenting me.

Things like: Grace, spread out beneath me, the faded green wool pooling all around her. My fingertips tracing up the bare skin of her legs, dipping under the hem and disappearing from view. Her lips parting on a sigh, head tilting back as my thumbs brush against black cotton.

These aren't fevered, shameful thoughts. This is *happening*, and I can barely think over the thud of my heartbeat in my ears. She's so soft and warm and welcoming, her arms lifting to loop around my neck. Those legs slide wider, and I rub against her again with my thumbs, her damp heat scorching through the cotton.

She wants this.

Fuck, *I* want this. So badly I can barely breathe.

"Grace." I yank my hands away and spread my palms on the rug, one on either side of her head. She blinks up at me, so trusting. "I want to kiss you first."

She snorts, brown eyes twinkling. "I should freaking hope so."

God. She's right. I'm doing this all out of order, getting muddled by how badly I want her, and this is the most important moment of my whole life so far. I need to get this right.

Because somehow, by some miraculous twist of fate, Grace broke down outside my cabin in this storm. She let me give her shelter, and now she's trusting me with even more. I won't waste a second of this.

The fire pops as I lower my head. Her lips press against mine, curving into a mischievous smile, and my chest aches as I kiss her a second time, deeper.

Am I doing this right?

If I speak, will it put her off?

Grace sucks on my tongue, and I let out a ragged groan. "You're going to kill me."

Knees hitch around my hips, holding me in place. "You can handle it," she murmurs against my neck.

And I don't know what I expected this would be like. More orderly, maybe? Instead it's hot and blurry and I keep losing track of my hands; I realize after ten minutes that I've been rocking my hips down against her, thrusting between the cradle of her thighs. It's shameless, but honest. I really am running on pure instincts, my body taking the reins.

I kiss Grace for the dozenth time, breathing hard against her damp lips. Could do this forever. Could die here with a smile on my face.

"Aiden," she whispers, her nails scratching at my beard. "Wanna do more?"

Yes I fucking do.

Immediately, a slideshow of images batter my brain. Things I want to do to Grace; places I want to touch her, lick her, *fuck* her. I want her bent over the arm of my sofa, my face buried between her cheeks. I want her on her knees, my cock sliding between her lips. I want to lay back on the rug beside the fire, lounging like an emperor, and feel her body sink down onto mine.

I won't take any of this for granted. And I won't push her too far.

"I could kiss you here." My palm flattens over the juncture of her thighs, pressing down on her through the sweater. Grace whimpers, rocking up into my touch. "What do you think?"

Her laugh is breathless. "Genius idea. Ten out of ten." Small hands bat at my shoulders, urging me down her body, and I tear myself away from the sweet heaven of her mouth.

Grace's pulse flutters beneath her jaw. I nibble her there.

Those small, round tits are heaving under the borrowed sweater. I kiss her there too, through the smoke-scented wool. Her breath hitches, her body writhing under mine, and I'm dying, I'm dying a slow, perfect death as I settle on my stomach, my shoulders between her thighs.

My cock is going to drill clean through the floorboards. I grit my teeth, shifting to get more comfortable.

"It's, um." Grace plucks at the hem of the sweater as I push it slowly up her thighs; she lifts her ass and lets me pull down her panties. "It's pretty intimate, isn't it? Kinda vulnerable. I mean, I figured it would be, but I—"

My teeth scrape against her hip bone and she squeaks, fingers weaving through my hair.

"You don't need to worry." My broken voice rumbles against her bare stomach, the muscles twitching against my lips. "I'll stop whenever you say."

A strained huff. "That's not what I meant."

"Then what—"

"I'm *embarrassed*, you dingus. It's been a long day, and no one's seen me down there before, and now I'm seriously second guessing my personal topiary choices."

"You're perfect." I cut Grace off, parting her with my thumbs. She's pink and wet and glistening. "Perfect," I repeat, voice hushed. And she must hear the awe in my voice, must believe me at last, because Grace melts against the rug with a sigh.

"Okay." Her nails scratch against my scalp, and I fight the urge to buck into her hand. "Okay, I'm ready. Do your worst, Aiden McRae."

* * *

"I—*ah*—I knew you had moves!"

I shake my head, my ears rubbing against the thighs clamped around my neck, and suck one of Grace's folds into my mouth.

These aren't moves. That makes it sound so cheap, like I'd do this for any woman who turned up at my cabin. No: this is nothing that I've ever done before, and now that I've met Grace, the thought of doing it with someone else is plain wrong.

It's her. All her. She brings this out of me; she's brought these instincts of mine online, with her mischievous grin and her prissy little clipboard and the shameless way she rocks her hips up, seeking more.

"Aiden!" Her breathless cries are music to my ears, and I welcome the sting when she pulls on my hair. I want Grace to drown out the thunder shaking the mountainside; I want the noises she makes to echo around my head for days to come.

This might be all I get. The thought slithers through my brain, emptying a bucket of cold water down my spine, but I keep going. Won't waste a second.

"Tell me what you like." My breath mists hot against her folds and I wedge both hands beneath her ass; I squeeze her cheeks as I lap at her clit. And I really do want to hear it, but Grace is too far gone to answer, moaning loudly, lost to the world.

Fine. Good. I'll take her where she needs to go—if it's the last goddamn thing I do, I'll get her there. I'll feel Grace come against my tongue, and I'll feel her body shudder under mine, and that will have to be enough. Once she's gone back to her normal life, that will be the memory.

"Aiden," Grace whimpers, tugging on my hair, and I slide one hand free, then work a finger inside her channel. Add a second, rubbing at her inner walls. I'm licking and rubbing and breathing hard, my neck aching like hell, and I'm too fucking hot this close to the fire, but I still don't want it to end.

It does, of course. The tension inside Grace winds tighter and tighter, her little noises getting more and more desperate. Then there's a moment, a space of a few heartbeats, where she's hovering. Dangling over the precipice, her whole body tensed.

"Come for me," I growl against her slickness, sucking on her clit. And Grace bows off the rug, her howl louder than the wolves as she twitches and shudders and sighs.

I lick her through it all. Commit every last gasp to memory.

And when she slumps against the cabin floor, grief slams into my chest.

It's over too fast. I'm not ready to be done with her yet—though maybe if I give her a minute to recover then start kissing her again, I can drag this out longer. Can steal another hour with our bodies entwined.

But when I rock back on my heels, wiping my mouth on my wrist, Grace winks at me from the rug. "We definitely need to add that to your Soulmate profile."

My heart crashes below the floorboards. Is that really all?

"Yeah," I agree, my voice hollow. "We should."

Grace

❧

I have no previous experience of The Aftermath, obviously, but so far it sucks. All the warm, happy feelings of an hour ago are long gone, and as I sit up by the fire, I shiver despite the wall of scorching heat by my side.

"Aiden."

He's pushing to his feet, expression stony, cheeks still flushed from his time spent buried between my thighs.

Oh, god. I'm still so slick and tingly down there. It felt amazing a few minutes ago, but now that the mood is gone, it's just uncomfortable. I pluck my panties off the rug nearby, heart tapping sickly against my ribs as I pull them back on.

This is the worst.

Did I do something wrong? Is my body secretly really weird down there?

Or is it that stupid joke I made about his Soulmate profile? No, it can't have been that. Because he *agreed* with me, like I wasn't joking at all, and oh god, is he really going to sign back up after this? Will I have to match Aiden McRae with other women?

Nuh-uh. No way. I have a freaking heart, damn it, and it's crumbling to ash at the mere thought. Someone else at Soulmate Express can take over his file.

"Is everything okay?" I wrap my arms around my legs and rest my chin on my knees. Still can't seem to get warm.

Aiden's stomping around the cabin, too busy to acknowledge my question. He clears up the leftovers from dinner and pauses by the log burner to stoke the fire; he pulls back a curtain to check on the storm.

Now that he's kept his distance for a few minutes, you'd never know anything happened between us at all. The blush has faded from his cheeks, and he's refastened his shirt buttons. Grace who?

"Aiden?" I sound miserable, even to my own ears.

Still peering through the dark glass out at the trees, he sighs, those broad shoulders dropping.

"Storm's still going." Would he want me to leave otherwise? Ouch. "You can take the bed. I'll sleep on the rug."

Ouch, ouch, ouch. I bite my lip to keep my face from crumpling.

"You, um." I clear my throat. "You shouldn't have to give up your bed. I'll sleep on the sofa."

"My austere sofa?" He turns to face me at last, humor flickering through those green eyes, but it doesn't last. "No, you won't be comfortable. And I don't mind the floor."

Neither do I, damn it. I don't care where I freaking sleep, I just want this horrible tension between us to be gone. I want to be able to swallow without this stupid lump in my throat, and I want Aiden to look at me again like he did before we tumbled into each other's arms.

Softly. Like he was glad I was here.

"You could join me in the bed?" I rasp, because apparently my bruised heart can't take a hint.

Aiden shakes his head, and I squeeze my arms tighter around my shins. Like I could crumple myself into a tiny ball and escape these sickly feelings.

"Go ahead." He nods at the bed in the corner. The soft-looking, freshly laundered bed. The one I declared *very inviting* not so long ago. "I'll wake you at first light."

Yeah. To get me out of here as soon as possible.

I push upright, swaying on my feet.

* * *

Can't sleep. It's not really a surprise, what with the last remnants of the storm moaning outside, and the unfamiliar bed, and the cold stranger lying with his arms folded on his chest by the fire. I toss and turn for a long time, huffing and puffing into Aiden's pillow, before finally giving up and swinging my feet onto the floor.

His breaths are coming slow and steady. Even in his sleep, his poor throat sounds sore. When I kissed his neck earlier, I felt the rigid line of a scar beneath his beard. What happened to him?

Guess I'll never have a chance to ask.

Shivering against the cool air, I tiptoe across Aiden's cabin, lips pressed in a firm line. I'm still dressed in his green sweater, the fabric swamping my body, and I'm grateful for it as I peel the front door open and slip out onto the deck.

Cold. That's what hits me first: a wall of frosty air, slapping my cheeks awake and delving between the strands of my mussed hair, then seeping through the tiny pores of my sweater. It's like sliding into a tub of icy bathwater. I shiver, wrapping my arms around my waist, but I don't really mind. It's refreshing.

Dawn's not here yet, but it can't be far off, because the first stars are winking out and there's a pale line of light on the horizon. All around Aiden's cabin, broken tree branches are strewn like confetti, and streams of rainwater course down the dirt driveway.

My rental car is where I left it, painted metal gleaming under the moonlight.

For a hot second, I think about sneaking back inside and grabbing my clothes. Or maybe not even doing that—maybe tugging off my borrowed socks and running across the wet dirt barefoot, then piling into the car, stolen sweater and all. I left the key in the ignition. There's a tiny chance it might work.

Then I could roll out of here and never feel this clammy despair ever again. Never see those moss green eyes, hard with indifference.

Tempting. Very tempting.

But I guess I'll never know whether my great escape would've worked, because the cabin door swings open behind me and a shaft of golden light spills over the deck.

Aiden's footsteps are quiet. He must know all the creakiest floorboards by heart.

"How's it looking?" he asks.

I wave an arm at the wreckage surrounding his cabin. "Messy. Guess mountain storms are like that."

Aiden grunts. "Guess so."

We stand in awkward silence for a minute. Then two. Every

second that falls away, my stomach twists tighter until I can't stand it for another moment.

"Well, then." Ugh, I've got my Little Miss Professional voice back on, but I don't know how to stop it. Sometimes I want to slap myself. "Better head back into the warm."

Aiden steps aside and lets me through, one arm stretched over my head in the doorway, and if I suck in a hungry breath of him as I pass…

I know, I know. It's pathetic.

But hey. I'm only human.

Aiden

∼⟨𝓎𝓸𝓎⟩∼

At dawn, I get her car working in five minutes flat. There's barely anything wrong with it, though Grace blinks at me like I'm a mechanical god, a tartan blanket wrapped around her shoulders.

The ghost of yesterday's hope stirs in my gut, but I tamp it down. She's already decided she's leaving. She ducked into my bathroom with a pile of her dried clothes after breakfast, then came out wearing that skirt suit again.

Sure, it's creased to hell and smells like smoke after drying by the fire overnight. But it feels like a message: the laughing, intimate, joyful Grace from dinner last night is gone. A distant memory. Professional matchmaker Grace is back.

Watch out, world.

"Thank you for letting me stay." She's nothing but smooth politeness as she folds the tartan blanket and hands it back. She folded my sweater like that too, and left it in a pile on the coffee table with those red knitted socks balled on top. When she wasn't looking, I spread my palm over the pile of fabric, but it was too late. Her body heat was gone. "It's been... um."

Yup. It's *been.*

"Take care, Grace." There are a thousand other things I want to say to her, a hundred reasons I want to give for her to stay, but for once, the pain in my throat is getting the better of me. Can't choke out the words. "Go slowly on the mountain roads."

She nods, face ashen. "I will."

And I should reassure her, should make her feel better about the drive down to Cloudy Lake, but as I tug her car door open, I can't speak at all.

I already gave her the number for Mountain Rescue. Already packed her rental car with any supplies she might need. She'll be fine—she's never needed me before, and she won't start now.

I hover by her open door as she settles in the seat, willing her to ask me to come with her. To see her off safely.

"Well," Grace says. "Bye, then."

Yeah. Fuck. I slam the door a little harder than I should, wincing at my own clumsiness, then lean down so she knows I'm not pissed off at *her.* The car window hums down.

"Take the bends extra slow. If there's a tree in the road, don't try anything fancy, just come straight back here. Okay?"

"Okay. And Aiden..."

I frown at the hollow of her throat as she chooses her words. Grace keeps swallowing, like this is hard for her too. And her pulse flutters beneath her jaw, like her heart is racing at a hundred miles an hour.

Is she alright? Is she falling apart too?

"I'm going to reassign your Soulmate file to someone else. No offense." I blink at her, and it's like my hearing suddenly sharpens, everything coming back into focus. Sounds are louder; colors are bright.

Grace is stiff in the driver's seat, her fingers plucking at her smoky skirt. She's speaking normally, but her eyes are fixed an inch or two above my shoulder, like she can't look me in the eye when she says this. "I'm not sure I can take it. You know. Emotionally."

Brown eyes dart to mine, then away, but not before I've seen the way they're brimming with pain. Her mouth curves up on one side, and her joke sounds hollow. "I promise it's not about my perfect record. I'm just a giant baby."

Fuck. This.

Grace squeaks as I yank her door open, reaching past her to unclip her seat belt. "What are you—"

It's so easy to lift her out of the car, even in her pencil skirt. She's so light, the wind could snatch her from my arms.

I tighten my hold on her. Not likely.

"What are you talking about?" I demand, setting her down and taking her shoulders. Grace glares up at me like I've lost my mind, but she's gripping onto my elbows just as hard. "You don't want me signed up for another match? Is that what you're saying?"

Her eyes narrow, and I swear, if a lightning bolt struck me down in this second, I'd blame it on Grace. She's a pint-sized package of wrath. "Of course I don't. What's the matter with you, Aiden?"

With *me*? "You're the one who said that shit about my Soulmate profile! I could still taste you on my lips, Grace. You'd saturated my fucking beard. I don't want to stay signed up, and I already told you that. You're the one who's desperate to match me with another goddamn woman."

I break off, chest heaving. Jesus Christ, I could tear a tree out by the roots. I could sprint up to the mountain summit, fueled by frustration alone.

How can she think that? How can she possibly think I want someone else? It couldn't be more obvious if I painted it on my forehead: I want *her*. Grace. And if I can't have her, I don't want anyone.

It's not rocket science. And she's a smart girl, so I know she gets it.

"I… you…" Grace clings to my elbows, lost for words.

…So maybe not. Maybe I think I've been obvious, mooning after her with hearts in my eyes, but that's not enough. Maybe I need to be crystal clear.

The sky tilts overhead as I bend down, pressing my shoulder against Grace's stomach. She yelps, scrabbling at my shirt, and I hide a smile as I straighten up with my girl slung over my back. The morning breeze ruffles my hair, scented with wet rock and pine, and I feel brand new. Wide awake for the first time in months; scrubbed clean by the storm.

"You can leave if you want," I call, marching back toward the cabin. She smacks my ass, cursing loudly for me to put her down. "This ain't a kidnapping. But if you're asking what I want, it's this. It's you coming back inside, and staying for good this time."

Dangling behind me, Grace falls quiet.

The wooden steps creak beneath my boots. When I open the door, it smells like smoke and chili and paint and fresh mountain air. It smells like home.

I carry my girl over the threshold, and I pray that she'll stay.

* * *

This time, when Grace falls back on my bed, I follow her down, my hands sinking into the deep red covers on either side of her head. Strands of her silky brown hair tickle my knuckles.

You could join me, she said last night, and I could kick my own ass for being so stubborn. For refusing to hear what she was trying to tell me, calling for me to join her in the bed.

No more. We're both done being bone-heads. "This okay?" I ask, and Grace nods so fast that her teeth click together. She's gripping two handfuls of my shirt, squeezing tight like I might lurch away from her again.

No chance. This is it.

Me and her. It's finally happening.

"The first time might not rock your world," I warn her, trying to make my own peace with that fact. "But I'm a quick study. I'll get you moaning for me soon enough."

If it's the last thing I do, I will feel this woman come around my cock. So help me god.

Grace hiccups a laugh. "I believe you."

And I can see that she does, can read it in her big doe eyes, and it fills me up so much that I might explode. I duck my head and trail kisses down her throat; I shift until my hips rest in the cradle of her thighs. Nearby in the log burner, the fire's burned down to a few glowing embers.

"Aiden?"

Her voice is strained, her hands plucking at the back of my shirt. I lift my head, my thoughts already tangled up from her vanilla scent. "Yeah, sweetheart?"

Grace bites her bottom lip and addresses the top button of my shirt. "This isn't a one time thing, right? You meant what you said out there? You really want me to stay here with you?"

Stay here.

Live here.

Marry me and have my babies. Whatever she's offering, that's what I want, and I try to show her with a deep, hungry kiss.

"I'll come to you if you prefer that." My words vibrate against her lips, and Grace's breath hitches before she kisses me back. "I'll find work in the city. Fuck you every night in your reading nook."

A scandalized gasp. "Not my *nook*."

"Yeah." Jesus, is making love always this fun? I can't stop grinning as we kiss and rock together, limbs tangled and cheeks flushed. "Is that what you want, Grace? A mail order groom?"

She snorts, and I bury my laugh in her hair. This can't be real. It can't be.

Feels too good. So light and warm, like my chest is full of embers.

"No," she says a few minutes later, sitting up to let me peel the shirt and blazer off her perfect body. "No, I don't want to go back to the city. God, you'd hate it. Let's stay here."

Her skirt rustles as I drag it down her thighs. Her olive skin goosepimples under my touch. "What about your job?"

Because I'm not blind. Grace loves her work; it was her whole world less than twenty four hours ago. And the last thing I want to do is make her unhappy—I want her to have zero regrets for choosing me.

"Maybe I can do outreach. Go knock on cabin doors for Soulmate Express." Grace chuckles, leaning up to flick open the buttons on my shirt. "We sure get enough sign-ups from around here. I've heard the locals call this place Mail Order Mountain."

Ha. Yeah, they do call it that. Used to drive me nuts.

But as my girl yanks my belt open, I have to admit: they're not wrong.

Grace

◦─◦❦◦─◦

Feeling Aiden's weight settle over me fills me with calm. Like finally, after years of feeling antsy and hollow and kind of weird without knowing why, everything is right with the world when his bare skin slides against mine. His heat; his pine-scent; his muscled chest dusted with brown hair. All of it makes my heart sing.

Honestly, he could suck at this and I don't think I'd care.

I don't tell him that, obviously. Why jinx myself?

"Grace," Aiden mutters, pressing kisses along my jaw. "Fuck, you're perfect. So perfect. And *mine*."

How possessive of him. I know the feeling, though. "Yup." My fingers weave through his coppery hair and tug lightly on the strands. "Likewise."

Aiden scoffs. "No shit."

Okay, so my mountain man is no poet, but it's impossible to miss the reverent way he strokes his palms down my body. Impossible not to arch up into his touch, gasping as he pinches my nipples and squeezes my waist. He scorches a tingling trail over my skin, and I'm aching. Slick and eager, my pulse thudding between my thighs.

What's a romantic way to tell him to fuck me already? I've wanted him so badly since the moment I saw him. My body has been on edge, wanting, *yearning.*

"Aiden." My legs part wider and I scratch my fingernails along the back of his neck. "I want you." His shuddering breath makes me bolder, and I bow off the mattress, cleaving against him. My teeth find his earlobe and nip the soft flesh. "I want you inside me."

"Jesus." He's rocking against me, his hard length rubbing through my folds. Coating himself in my slickness; making himself ready. Making me so desperate my teeth ache.

"Aiden," I snap, and his gruff laugh makes me scowl at the ceiling.

Not for long. It's impossible to be cranky when this man kisses me deeply, his tongue sliding against mine, shifting to line up with my entrance. I'm not really mad anyway, I'm eager, desperate—

"Oh, shit." I bite down on his shoulder, eyes burning as he presses the first inch inside me. It *stings.* I didn't realize it would sting like this. "Oh. Ow."

Above me, Aiden turns to stone. My stomach drops. Have I ruined this already? God, I'm such a wimp.

"No, no, no," I say, clutching at his shoulders as he kneels up and pulls my ass into his lap, the head of his cock still wedged inside me. "Don't stop. Please don't stop. I can handle it, I swear."

Aiden's frown could wither the strongest pine tree down to a shriveled twig. "I don't want you to handle it, Grace. I want you to enjoy it."

Yeah, well, obviously. And I'd like a million dollars and a talking pet cat.

I open my mouth to argue, but my words choke off when Aiden's thumb finds my clit.

...Oh.

He rubs me there, steady and gentle. Teasing me, softening me up, until the tension drains away and my legs sag open on his lap. I probably look nuts, probably look like some kind of lounging drunkard, but I don't care.

"Ngh," I say, hands clutching at the bed covers. My hips keep lifting, rising of their own accord, chasing his not-quite-enough touch, and Aiden smirks down at me.

"I've got you."

Yeah. Shit. He—*ah*—he really, really has. I'm slicker than I've ever been, my racing pulse pounding between my legs.

"You like that, Grace?" My fevered nodding makes his eyes burn hotter. He looks ready to swallow me whole. "Good girl."

Gah! I whimper, hips thrusting until he slides an inch deeper inside me. Aiden hisses between his teeth, but he stays still, thumb rubbing.

"I'm ready." I'm pleading shamelessly, smacking at his strong thigh, but I don't care. I *need* him. "I'm ready, Aiden. Do it. Keep—keep going. Fuck me."

The asshole hums, and ignores me completely. Rubs me in steady circles like he has all freaking day.

"Aiden!"

He's merciless, but I should have known. Should have figured he'd take no prisoners. Because Aiden McRae brings me off with singular focus, every ounce of his attention scorching over my body; he's deaf to my desperate wails. He touches and strokes and rubs me until I can't take anymore, until the partial intrusion of his cock is the world's most agonizing tease, until heat floods my body to the tips of my toes, and I stiffen on his lap and fall apart with a broken cry.

God.

My body clamps down on the head of his cock, trying to suck him deeper. Trying to feel full, damn it, but freaking Aiden waits for me to collapse before he crawls on top of me again.

"I hate you."

He grins and kisses me hard. "No, you don't."

It's easier this time. Smoother and softer. My body opens for him like it's the most natural thing in the world, like we're welcoming him home. My knees hitch around his waist, while my arms wrap around his neck.

We're sealed together. Blurring into one.

Finally.

Don't want this to stop. I never want this to end, and I'm embarrassed to admit that tears burn in my eyes as Aiden rocks into me, deeper, harder. He jerks back and goes still when he notices, his expression raw.

"It still hurts?"

I'm already shaking my head, already tugging him back down. "No." I sniffle against his neck. Wipe my eyes on his beautiful beard. "No, I'm just happy."

"Funny way to show it," he grumbles, but he's clutching me closer, still thrusting deep inside me. "Ah, fuck. Grace. Your body."

"I know." This is too good. The slick slide of him inside me makes my toes curl, and his rough grip on my breasts makes me sigh. I'm a humming livewire, throwing off sparks beneath him. "Keep going."

There's a real risk here that I will never go to work again. I'll forget to eat or sleep or function, because all I ever want to do is *this*, with Aiden, every minute of every damn day. I've found heaven, and it's with my mountain man buried between my legs.

After a while, the tempo changes. We get rougher, more urgent. Aiden squeezes my ass hard enough to leave a bruise, and I score his back with my fingernails.

"Turn over." He pulls out, hands trembling, but his grip is sure as he flips me over.

"I'm not a damn pancake."

His palm cracks against my ass. "Behave. Are you ready?"

I bury my laugh in the bed covers, raising my ass. And this time when he takes me, Aiden McRae freaking *owns* me. He shows no mercy, and he takes me hard and rough. When he wraps his fist in my hair, I let out a blissful sigh, and when he reaches around me to rub my clit, I curse louder than a sailor.

"Aiden! You—I'm going to—"

"Do it." He grinds the words between his teeth. "Fuck, Grace. Give it to me."

It's something else, falling apart with him buried inside me. With his thick shaft wedged deep in my body, swelling and pulsing as he follows me over the edge. We both shudder and gasp, letting out hoarse groans that echo round the cabin.

I'd be self conscious, if he weren't just as far gone.

"Jesus," Aiden heaves out two minutes later, spread out on my back with his face buried in my hair. He's still inside me, his spend trickling down my thigh. "That was…"

"Yeah," I agree, breathless. "It was. Now get off, you big lump."

He rolls to the side and drags me against his chest. Tucks

my hair behind my ear and presses a kiss to my neck.

I'm sweaty and sticky. So happy I could whoop.

So *this* is the mountain man experience.

* * *

Ten months later

I'm tapping away at my laptop, perched on a high stool at the bar, when a wall of solid heat comes up behind me. Biting back a smile, I shift on my seat and lean back until my shoulder blades hit a strong chest, still typing feverishly all the while.

All around the room, locals laugh together in booths and swig from beer bottles; they stomp pine needles from their boots as they file through the front door. Over in the corner, someone coaxes fuzzy Elvis songs from the jukebox.

"Hey," Aiden says into my hair, his deep, broken voice making me shiver. "It's dark out. Is Soulmate Express making you work overtime?"

I snort, blowing a strand of dark hair out of my face. My fingers blur over the keyboard, and as I work, it's like the whole Cloudy Lake bar fades away, the chatter going quiet and the clink of glasses muffled. There's only me, Aiden, the fresh orange juice I just ordered, and this freaking perfect match I'm making. I am on fire.

"No," I say at last when Aiden's question registers in my brain. "They're not making me do anything. But you have to see this pairing, Aiden. They're, like, made for each other and they've never even met—"

"One day," Aiden murmurs against my neck, his palm sliding around to cup my small baby bump, his thumb stroking me through my sweater, "one day soon, you're going to slow down, Grace. You're going to take time off, and let me rub your feet in the evenings, and lord it over me that you're creating our baby inside you. Boss me around like you should."

"Yeah, yeah." I wave a hand, still typing with the other. "Miracle of pregnancy, yada yada. I *do* rest, but this match—"

"It'll keep."

"It's love, you boob!" I finally stop typing to swing around on my stool, looping my arms around my husband's neck. He watches me calmly, green eyes crinkling with amusement, and braces his hands on my hips. The sounds of the bar fade back in, Elvis crooning from the corner. "How would you feel if we'd taken an extra nine months to find each other?"

"Very sad." Aiden leans closer, smirking beneath his coppery beard. "But don't pretend this isn't about your perfect record."

Ugh. Please. This is not about my record.

Not entirely, anyway.

Although... I chew on my bottom lip, glancing over at the dark windows. My shoulders are getting pretty stiff, and my eyes are dry from staring at a screen. Maybe I should call it a night.

Aiden grins when I flip my laptop closed, then drags a stool next to mine, folding his strong arms on the bar. He peers at my orange juice, leaning in for a quick sniff.

"Hey!" I swipe my glass away, sucking on the straw. "Your pregnant wife is not drinking booze in a bar, Aiden McRae."

"No." A big hand reaches over and kneads my stiff shoulder. "She's just working herself into the ground, all for the love of two strangers."

Yeah, okay. Guilty as charged, so maybe I *will* take some time off. Like Aiden says... it'll keep.

We could hole up in the cabin together. I could eat snacks and watch Aiden paint, distracting him while he works on his fancy commissions. Or maybe he'll paint me again.

He does that, sometimes. There are dozens of canvases with my face and body on them already—enough for a whole exhibition.

Damn, he'd better not show those in a gallery. Those poses were private.

"Grace." A panicked voice filters through the chatter of the bar. I turn and find Nina, a young woman I've been working with in the Cloudy Lake coffee shop lately. We keep each other company most mornings, swapping jokes over our laptops. Nina's good fun, especially once she starts ranting about her horrible boss. "Grace. Oh my god, what have you done?"

I frown at my friend, taking in her wild black hair, scraped up in a lopsided bun; her flushed cheeks and her wide gray eyes. Nina normally dresses in cute skirts and blouses, but tonight it looks like she ran to the bar in a sweater and old leggings.

"Um." I rattle the ice in my glass. "It's just orange juice."

"No." She's still staring at me with those wide, horrified eyes. Beside me, Aiden tenses on his stool, inching closer. So protective, even though Nina's no threat. "No—the match. I'm talking about my match."

Oh, yeah. Nina's one of my best success stories. She'd been lonely and bored in Cloudy Lake, and though things got better once we started hanging out, it was the Soulmate match I made for her that really turned things around. She's been swapping messages with a mountain man, telling him her secrets and getting closer. Sighing about him over lattes.

She's been so happy, she's been floating everywhere instead

of walking. Even her rants about her boss have been delivered with a smile.

"Did something happen?" My stomach drops at the thought. The mountain can be dangerous, especially in the colder months. Did her match have an accident? "Nina?"

"It's him," she hisses, digging her fingers into her hair. Her messy bun lists even further to the side. "You matched me with *him*. How could that happen? Did you know?"

"Know what?" I glance at Aiden and he shrugs. Okay, so this is confusing as hell for him, too. That's a relief. "Who's him?"

"My boss." Nina drags both palms down her cheeks, stretching her face out with frustration, and I'd laugh if she weren't so distraught. "You matched me with my boss! We've been messaging, Grace. I told him things! Private things! I even bitched about my work, and I confessed all these secrets, and now I—"

Nina clams up, bright red with mortification. There's a long pause, and then Aiden slides off his stool.

"I'll, uh. I'll give you two a minute."

I glare at his broad shoulders as he pushes through the crowd. Traitor.

When I guide Nina onto the empty stool, she lets out a wobbly sigh. At least she's still here, right? Talking to me? And I can fix this. Not for my record—for my friend.

"I'll match you with someone else," I say in my most soothing voice. But Nina's face crumples, and she shakes her head fast.

"No! No, I don't want anyone else. I just… I wish none of this ever happened. This is so humiliating." She collapses onto her folded arms, black bun flopping forward. "He was so different in his messages," she says, voice muffled. "Like a whole other man. So kind and funny and interested in me. For a second there, I thought…"

My mouth twists as I rub her shoulder blades. Nodding at the bartender, I call for another orange juice and the beer Nina likes. Traitor McRae can order his own.

"I'm so sorry, Nina. But this will be ancient history soon, I promise. And if your boss is weird about it—"

"He doesn't know. We haven't exchanged real names yet."

"Then how—?"

"He sent a photo of his desk and the project he's working on. I recognized it. There's even the World's Worst Boss mug I gave him for the holidays last year."

I open my mouth, then close it again. Nope. Not going near that.

"I want what *you* have," Nina grumbles, sitting up when her beer arrives. "You and Aiden. I want the fairy tale, you know?"

"Sure."

And I really do. Some days, I can't believe how good things are. I wake up beside my gorgeous, bearded husband in our cozy cabin and pinch myself to make extra sure it's all real.

"You'll find that." I try to sound confident, even though my record is officially no longer perfect. "I have good intuition about this stuff, and you're going to find love, Nina."

She swigs from her beer bottle, her expression sour.

A warm hand settles against the small of my back, and some of the tension bleeds from my body. I lean into my husband, offering him a quick smile.

"You girls got it sorted?" Aiden's watching Nina with concern.

"We will," I say quickly. "It's going to be fine. Right, Nina?"

She shudders out a long breath and nods, then starts peeling the label off her beer. Her eyes are bright, like she's trying not to cry.

Aiden leans in, his lips grazing my ear, and speaks low so only I can hear. "Fuck, I'm glad you broke down outside my cabin. I forgot how brutal it is out there."

Tell me about it. I nod and press a quick kiss to Aiden's scarred throat, thanking all my lucky stars for that well-timed storm and that shitty rental car. Then I start to chat with Nina, trying to draw her onto nicer topics, but all the while I lean back on my stool until I'm sealed against Aiden's chest.

He warms me.

Anchors me.

Steadies me with one hand on my waist.

Nina watches us together, and she looks wistful. But I will see her happy again, damn it, because I know one thing she doesn't: her match score with her boss was perfect. *Perfect.*

Those numbers don't lie.

There's hope for Nina yet.

* * *

"That was rough." Aiden stamps his boots on the deck before leading the way inside our cabin, shrugging off his winter jacket before crossing to the log burner. He crouches and starts building a fire, his strong thighs pushing against his jeans, and I bite my lip as I watch him from the door.

I'm lucky. So, so lucky.

I feel pretty damn grateful, and I'm inclined to show it.

The door swings shut behind me. I unwind my scarf and peel off my puffy coat. My steps are muffled by thick socks as I cross the cabin to my husband, weaving between the coffee table and a stack of blank canvases.

"Sucks that Nina wasted her time—"

Aiden cuts off when I drop to my knees by his side, hiding a smile as I reach for his belt. He's a stone statue, arms raised in surrender, his chest already heaving as I tug on the leather.

"I don't think it was a waste. My spidey senses are tingling."

"Oh yeah?" Aiden asks, winded, as I unzip his jeans and draw out his hard cock, so familiar to me after all these months.

He's warm and firm against my palm, thick and ruddy. When I squeeze his shaft, I can feel his pulse thud against my fingertip. Aiden groans, hips twitching forward into my grip.

My hair swings forward as I lean down, lips parting. The first lick is salty, and I smile at my husband's pained hiss. He's breathing hard, and I love that—I love how he comes undone for me.

"They'll be fine," I say, my lips grazing his length. Glancing up at him, I wink. "It's fate."

III

Bossy Beard

Description

I'm falling in love with my mail order match.

Then I find out—he's my grumpy boss.

How could this happen? There are thousands signed up to Soulmate Express. Thousands who could have been my happy ever after.

Instead I've been writing to the grouchiest man I know. Telling him secrets, confessing my innermost dreams... complaining about my horrible boss.

Ugh.

This can't happen. I need to forget the dreamy man I've been writing to, and go on like everything is fine.

And my boss can *never* know he was matched with me.

Because he'd hate that... right?

Soulmate Express

D ear SomethingsGottaGive,

Good to hear from you. Glad I didn't scare you off with stories of getting car-jacked in the jungle and stalked by the mob. I have normal stories too, I promise. One day, I hope I'll tell you them in person.

In answer to your question… well, I'll be honest about why I signed up to the mail order match program, but I'm afraid you won't like it. The truth is: I'm tired of wanting someone I can't have. Is that a deal breaker for you?

Yours,

MrWrite

* * *

Dear MrWrite,

No, it's not a deal breaker.
  It's the most relatable thing I've ever heard.

Yours,

SomethingsGottaGive

Nina

I've thought about it from all angles and here's my conclusion: Merrick Bates was put on this earth to test my spirit. There's no other explanation.

Two years, I've worked for that jerk. Two years of his stupid, handsome face giving me that *look*, the one that says he knows I can do better and he expects me to try. Two years of scheduling his meetings and picking up his dry cleaning; of calling the best restaurants in the city and persuading them that yes, they really do want to offer take out, and while they're at it, please make sure no olives get within a meter radius of Merrick's plate.

I've worked dozens of late nights, swigging coffee after coffee, my hands shaking from the jitters, just so I could click 'send' on an email when he finally gave me the nod.

I've skipped parties and canceled trips. Sent thank you notes to his sources, copying his handwriting with my tongue poked between my teeth.

Then I moved out here. Followed Merrick to the freaking

mountains, trailing after him on sabbatical like an obedient puppy with a smartphone. I watched my jet-setting investigative journalist boss trade his sharp suits for flannel shirts; watched his clean shaven jaw grow a short beard—and the worst part of all is that his new look *suits* him.

He looks good, the asshole.

I mean, he always looks good. Catching sight of him is like a phantom punch to the chest, every single time. But tonight, as he yanks his cabin door open and frowns at me on his deck, he's so gorgeous in the fading light that I want to cry.

It's unearned, you know? People's outsides should look like their insides. And Merrick Bates has no business striding around this mountain like some kind of gentleman lumberjack, the wind tugging on his thick blond hair and his icy blue eyes scowling against the cold.

Whenever he leaves his Cabin of Isolation and comes down to Cloudy Lake, you can *hear* the panties sizzling off the local women—though he'd never deign to notice the effect he has. God, it's frustrating. Makes me want to gnaw on a tree branch like a beaver.

"You're late." His low voice is clipped. Steady eyes watch me, a strong hand holding the door open wide. Merrick is clad in a midnight blue shirt, and the way it hugs his broad shoulders makes my mouth go dry.

Late. To hand-deliver his dinner.

Right.

I suck in a deep breath and offer my horrible boss his take out container. With the soggy cardboard already cooling in my hands, we're a long way from the city.

"One black bean stir fry. You're welcome, sir."

His mouth twitches and he jerks his chin inside. I don't really want to come in—I'd rather tromp back down to the Cloudy Lake bar and sink a beer or two with my friend Grace and her husband—but that's the thing with asshole bosses. They don't care about your Friday night plans.

As I step inside the cabin, the warm air turns my cheeks pink. A fire pops in the log burner in the center of the room, and the cabin is simple but cozy. Patterned rugs cover the floorboards and bookshelves line the walls, and it smells like sawdust and cinnamon. There's a squashy sofa and a kitchenette. A bed I'm trying very hard not to stare at.

"Do you need anything else tonight, sir?"

Heat crawls up my neck as I play back my own words, wincing at how suggestive they sound, but Merrick doesn't bat an eyelid. He strides to the desk pushed against the far wall and sifts through a stack of papers.

It's probably never even crossed his mind—what it sounded like I was offering.

It's crossed mine, though. God help me, it's crossing mine right this second: the thought of my grumpy boss turning to face me, shadows playing across his handsome face as he folds his arms. The shift of his throat; the rise and fall of his chest. The way he'd say in that low, clipped voice: *Yes, Nina. Strip.* The possessive way he'd watch me pulling off my clothes one by one, staring at my tan skin and wild black hair with pure hunger.

A girl can dream, okay?

And there's no harm done, because Merrick rummages around on his messy desk, oblivious to my secret daydreams. Dark jeans hug the strong muscles of his thighs, his hips shifting as he searches the clutter, and my mouth twists as I consider the cold, hard truth: I, Nina Perez, am a pervert.

I don't even *like* this man. He's bossy and demanding, and he raises my blood pressure with a single sardonic glance.

And yet here I am, thinking mournfully that he'll never bend *me* over that desk, one large palm splayed over my back as he rumbles filthy promises of what he'll do to me. How he'll punish me for being two minutes late with his stupid black bean stir fry.

So sad. Such a waste of all these tingly feelings.

Thank god for my mail order match. I'm finally, *finally* moving on from my crush on this jerk and talking to a decent man. One who I feel a real connection with; one who truly understands me.

Maybe one who'll bring *me* dinner on a Friday night, and who'll curl up with me on the sofa near the fire.

One who'll tell me to strip.

"Just a second, Nina." Merrick's voice drifts across the cabin, cutting over the soft rustle of paper. "I had it an hour ago."

Sure he did.

It's funny. This man is military-strict with everything else, including his schedule and his body. He runs exactly five miles each morning, even here in the mountains where there are cougars and bears, and god forbid I forget to add an appointment to his calendar. Even when he gets caught up with work and orders take out for dinner, it's never pizza. Strictly vegetables. He's more rigid than titanium, and yet his writing desk always looks like a hurricane blew through.

Everyone has a secret messy side, I guess.

It's kind of cool that I get to see his.

Merrick curses quietly, still sifting through his landslide of paper, and I stroll over the rugs to stand by his side. This close, I can kid myself that I can feel his body heat through my clothes. He smells like soap and mint and fresh mountain air, and I wonder idly how his neck would taste if I licked him.

"What are we looking for?"

Merrick blows out a harsh breath, shaking his head. "I made a list earlier of articles I want you to source for my research. It was right here."

Ha. I bet it was.

I hum, flicking at a toppled stapler. "So how's the book coming?"

The fire hisses in the burner, a log collapsing with a dull thump. My boss sounds sour. "It's not."

The whole reason we came out here, trading city conveniences for starry skies and patchy WiFi, is so Merrick can write his book. A big statement of a book; his magnum opus on corruption and corporate greed. The book that will cover his life's work as an investigative journalist and launch him into the non fiction charts. The book that will take his career to the next level.

Guess that'd give anybody writer's block. So much pressure.

A raunchy slideshow of all the ways I could help him relax flickers across my mind's eye—things like pushing him against the desk and dropping to my knees, or tackling him to the rug and straddling his hips—but I say nothing, fiddling with a loose thread on my coat sleeve.

Such. A. Pervert.

If I were smart, I'd have quit this job a long time ago. Taken my inappropriate crush and my poor, battered heart far away from the man beside me. Fled to someplace where his daily dismissal can't sting my insides. I *know* that, and yet every time I think about it, every time I start looking for other jobs...

I can't do it.

119

It's like this man anchors me. Whenever I think about never seeing him again, something vital inside me revolts.

Tragic.

It's okay, though. That's what the mail order bride program is for: a fresh start, far away from Merrick Bates. A chance at *requited* love for a change, with a man who can't resist my charms. Just thinking about MrWrite makes me stifle a smile.

"It's not funny," Merrick mutters, still flipping through his piles of notes. His hands are strong, the knuckles squared.

"Agree to disagree, sir."

My boss huffs and slants me a look before continuing his search. We do this dance at least once a week: he loses something on his bombsite desk, and I wait around and pointedly say nothing. He gets cranky and I try not to laugh. Rinse and repeat.

Again, the slideshow batters my brain with all the ways this could go differently. You know, if my boss saw me as a woman rather than as a planner on legs. Urgent kisses and fingernails raked down his back. My bra bouncing off the window pane.

I mean, I'm relying on my imagination here. It's not like I have any real life experience to go on.

"Your stir fry will get cold."

"Nina," he says, exasperated.

"I'm just saying. I carried that all the way from town."

"Such a hero," Merrick mutters. "*You* eat it, Nina. If your stomach growls any louder, you'll attract bears."

Ass.

But I have a longstanding policy of never turning down free food, so I scoop up his take out container and wander over to the kitchenette in search of a fork. The counters are clean and orderly; the utensils sparkle in their drawer. It's just Merrick's desk that gets the hurricane treatment—the rest of the cabin is spotless. What a weirdo.

Would he be orderly in bed? Or would his wild side come out there, too?

Has he *ever* thought about me that way? Even once? I sag against the counter, digging through the steaming carton of vegetables, and try to breathe past the tightness in my chest.

It's getting worse. This god-awful crush. It used to be my naughty little secret, something that made me feel all warm and gooey inside, but lately I've been thinking that the word 'crush' is literal.

It's flattening me. Squeezing out all my air.

I don't know how much longer I can go on like this.

"Found it." Over by the desk, Merrick snatches up a piece of paper, waving it like a flag. He prowls across the cabin to my side, folding the list neatly and tucking it in my coat pocket.

"Congratulations," I tell him around a mouthful of broccoli.

Merrick grunts and tugs open the cutlery drawer, grabbing his own fork then raiding the carton in my hand. His big fingers cover mine, steadying the container between us, and my pulse slows to an agonizing thud until Merrick lets go, a mushroom speared on his fork.

I suck in a deep breath as he turns away, my head spinning.

Can't keep doing this. I need to get away.

As I step out onto the deck five minutes later, the sunset turning the sky crimson through the trees, Merrick's list crinkles in my coat pocket. The corner of the paper jabs my hip through the fabric.

MrWrite, I remind myself, my boots thudding down the cabin steps. Soon, Merrick Bates will be ancient history to me. A fever dream.

My mail order match is my future.

* * *

Impatient, I toss my scarf on the foot of my bed, marching straight to the rickety desk pushed against the window. My lodgings are in the center of Cloudy Lake, overlooking the cobbled town square, and the distant sound of Friday night revelers drifts up to my bedroom.

I could go out there. Could join in with the fun.

Instead, I lever open my laptop, drop into the wooden chair, and log in to Soulmate Express.

It's been a few days since I last heard from MrWrite, but maybe the universe will hear my plea. I need a win tonight, need a sign that things are changing for me and soon I'll know love. Real love.

One unread message.

"Thank god," I mutter, clicking on my inbox. The universe has my back after all. And as I scan MrWrite's latest message, reading his story about a trip to Prague and his questions for me, a goofy smile stretches over my face.

Yeah. This is the man for me. I'm sure of it.

He's so different from the grouchy boss I spend my days pining after. MrWrite is charming and kind; he answers every question I ask and takes an interest in me too.

There's an attachment. A photo that the patchy internet is taking forever to load. I drum my nails on the table, chewing on my lip as I wait, and curiosity burns in my chest like a hot coal.

I asked for a photo from MrWrite's work. A sneak peek at his natural habitat. We're not allowed to exchange selfies, not yet, but I figured as long as we stayed anonymous, it wouldn't be cheating too badly. You can learn a lot about a man by his environment, right?

The photo loads. I blink, my body flashing icy cold, then burning hot.

No.

No way.

...*No.*

"Shit," I whisper through numb lips. "*Shit.*"

Because I know that desk, though it's tidier in the photo. I stared at those paper stacks less than thirty minutes ago. I've studied that whorl in the wood grain; I flicked that stapler. And there, in the corner of the desk, is the World's Worst Boss mug I gave Merrick last winter.

MrWrite.

I—I thought my match was an author! Or a poet or a screenwriter, or literally anything but my boss. Merrick Bates signed up to Soulmate Express? It's not possible. He doesn't have a romantic bone in his flawless body. And...

I was right there. Waiting for him for the last two years.

Jealousy churns my stomach, and I feel sick. So sick.

Behind me, my chair clatters to the floor as I yank open the bedroom door, charging out into the night. I need Grace and I need answers, and I need a beer.

Lots of beer.

Soulmate Express

D ear SomethingsGottaGive,

Haven't heard from you for a while. Is everything okay? If the sight of my messy desk scared you off… well, I'm ashamed to say that it's usually much messier.

A man can change, though. Hope to hear from you again.

Yours,

MrWrite

* * *

Dear MrWrite,

Sorry! No, it wasn't the desk. I'm, uh—leaving the country. Going away for a long, long time.

It's nothing you did. And I wish I could say "Hope you find a

new match!" without dying a little inside, but I can't so I won't.
  Good luck with everything.

Yours,

SomethingsGottaGive

Merrick

"We're walking and talking today." I stride past my assistant, her hand raised to knock on the cabin door I just flung open. "Some fresh air will help me think."

God, I hope so, because this book might actually kill me. Every time I think I'm making progress, every time I nail my argument down, a new idea slams into my brain in the middle of the night. I greet each morning sat up in bed, scrawling ideas in a notebook until a pink dawn stains the sky through my window, and by the time I sit down to my laptop to work, my fingers are stiff with cramp.

That's not the only reason we're walking today, of course. Mostly, I want to put some color back in Nina's cheeks.

There's something off about her lately. She seems tired. Beaten down by life.

I don't like it.

"Great," my assistant says now, her voice flat as she catches the dictaphone I toss at her. She trails me back down the cabin steps, moving much slower than I did. "I love our field trips. Tell me, Merrick: have you ever considered getting a dog?"

Ha. "You're better company, Nina."

She grumbles something under her breath, but it sounds like "Ass."

"A dog couldn't hold my dictaphone, either."

Reaching my side, Nina shoves at my shoulder, her mouth tugging up in a reluctant grin. And my heart jolts at the sight of it, my pulse thudding faster in my veins, but that flash of the old Nina is gone as soon as it came.

Then we're back to slumped shoulders and shadows under her eyes. She squints at the treeline, bundled up in leggings and winter boots and a wine red knitted dress. A puffy gray jacket and a fluffy blue scarf.

"You look warm," I rasp.

It's the only safe thing I can tell her, because I'm not about to tell my young assistant that she looks so fucking gorgeous I could howl. That I want nothing more than to press her up against the nearest tree, and to unwrap her layer by layer until her bare skin pebbles in the frosty morning air. That if I can't make her smile, I could at least make her moan.

So help me god, I will never be *that* boss.

Nina deserves better. She deserves an employer she can trust, and to feel respected at work, and a man who's not a decade older than her, too.

"Come on." Nina won't meet my eyes, but she clicks the dictaphone on with a flourish. Her puffy jacket sleeve rustles as she moves, and the air smells like pine sap and moss. "Get to work, Mr Bates."

Fine. I lead her away from my cabin, down the mountain path, and try to put my mysterious assistant from my mind.

* * *

See, the thing about Nina is that she'll never confess what's wrong. She's chatty about superficial stuff, always happy to tell a funny story or give her vote on what we should order for dinner when we work late, but when you try and go deeper than that, the girl's a steel vault.

Back when I first interviewed her for the job, I liked that about her. Figured she'd be trustworthy and that she'd keep my sources safe; that she'd never gossip and risk my work.

And that's all true, but fuck, I wish sometimes Nina would give me a tiny glimpse at what she's really thinking. At the thoughts whirling behind those soulful gray eyes. She's a locked box, and I want in.

"So." For a man who has interviewed thousands of sources, I suck at small talk. "Do you like the mountain life?"

We're perched on two giant boulders at the side of the path, catching our breath after a steep incline. Nina leans back on her palms, her cheeks bright pink as she shakes her head, gulping down air. The dictaphone lays beside her on the boulder, switched off.

"No. Hell no. Way too much cardio."

I grunt. "You sure about that, Perez?"

Because I've seen the soft, wistful look that creeps into her eyes sometimes when she's staring out at the mountains. I've seen the gleeful way she builds the fire in my wood burner, prodding at the logs with a poker, and I've wondered more than once whether she'd be tempted by any of the gruff mountain men around here.

Fuck, I'd hate that. She wouldn't be the first, though.

The locals call it Mail Order Mountain for a reason. Hell, I nearly found my own match through Soulmate Express—back before I scared her off with my clutter.

Probably for the best. I felt a draw to SomethingsGottaGive, no doubt about it, but the cranky girl next to me could crook a finger and I'd come running.

"Oh, I'm sure," Nina says, counting off her reasons on her fingers. "Back home, I live two doors down from the best Thai restaurant in the city. I can stream a movie without needing three hours to let it buffer. And if I'm ever bored, I can head down to the street at any hour, and I am *guaranteed* to witness something bizarre."

"No wolves, though."

She snorts, shaking her head. "Don't be so sure. I've seen weirder in the launderette at two AM."

I duck my chin, hiding a smile, and then I can't hold it back any longer. I ask the question that's been gnawing at me, nibbling away at my insides.

"What's wrong, Nina?"

She sucks in a soft breath and goes quiet. There's nothing but the breeze rustling the trees, and distant bird calls. The scrape of my boot as I shift against the boulder.

"I'm fine."

She doesn't sound fine. Nina's fiddling with a loose thread on her jacket sleeve, her voice all high-pitched and hoarse. I scrub a hand over my beard, and I've never felt so fucking useless. At least if a grizzly bear burst through the trees, I could throw myself in front of her; I could try to scare it off. I could do *something*. But this?

"Tell me, Nina. Please."

She sighs loudly, folding over her bent knees. Her eyes flick to me, then away, and when she speaks, I barely hear the words muffled in her puffy jacket sleeves. "Have you heard of Soulmate Express, sir?"

I stiffen.

Lie, a voice hisses in the back of my head. Fuck, she can't know I was on there. Then she'll want to know why, and Nina's smart. There's no way she won't see the truth splashed all over my face: that I signed up to escape my feelings for her.

But: "Yeah," I mutter, because I'm an idiot who's incapable of lying to this woman. "Yeah, I've heard of it."

Has she found a mail order match, then?

Kill me now.

Sure enough: "I had a match." Nina buries her face deeper in her sleeves, her nose turning pink from the cold. I shift closer, straining to hear each muffled word, and god, I feel sicker than my first teenage hangover. "I liked him a lot. But it didn't work out."

Thank Christ.

I force myself to nod. "That's a shame. What happened?"

Gray eyes narrow on me, and then Nina's sitting up, shoulders stiff. "Oh, you just assume that I was the problem? Some men actually like me, Merrick Bates—"

I hold up both palms, alarmed. "Of course I don't think you were the problem. God, Nina, who wouldn't want you?"

Silence.

Complete, strained silence.

We stare at each other, my hands raised, her eyes wide. We're frozen in this tableau of horror, and I would actually love it if a grizzly bear found us now. I'd go to my cuddly death with open arms.

"Let's go," I say when it becomes clear that a well-timed predator is not coming. Sliding off the boulder, my bones jar as I hit the dirt. "We need to work."

Work. Walk. Make some headway on this chapter.

And pretend I didn't just shove my whole hiking boot into my mouth.

Soulmate Express

Dear MrWrite,

Hey, it's me. I know we haven't spoken for a while and you've probably found another match by now, but I want to be extra clear: It wasn't you. *I* was the problem, okay? My stuff. And I hate the idea of you second-guessing yourself, or wondering where you went wrong.

You didn't. You were great, and I loved being matched with you.

Okay, hope that helps.

Yours,

SomethingsGottaGive

* * *

Dear SomethingsGottaGive,

Thanks for your message. I appreciate it.

Please don't worry about me, though—sure, without your lovely distraction, I'm doomed to pine after a woman I can't have, and yes, this need for her is eating me up from the inside. But I have my work, and I found a cabin for sale out here in the mountains. Maybe I'll stay here forever and become a cryptid.

She's my assistant. Did I ever tell you that? I'm her boss, and I spend most of my time daydreaming about bending her over the nearest piece of furniture. So don't feel too sorry for me, that's all I'm saying. I've got a one way ticket to hell.

Yours,

MrWrite

Nina

I burst into the Cloudy Lake bar in a flurry of damp black hair and fluffy blue scarf tails. Normally, I like to pretend that I have my shit together, but I saw MrWrite's message right after my evening shower, and I have no idea which clothes I threw on. I probably look like a crazed rag doll.

My heart pounds out a frantic rhythm as I weave between tables and dodge tonight's drinkers. As far as I can tell, this place is just called 'the bar'. There's a wooden sign on the building above the door, but the letters are too faded to read and I've never heard anyone call it by another name.

Who cares, right? The sky is falling.

"Grace," I wheeze, and my legs are numb as I stagger across the crowded room. She's here, tucked in a corner booth with her laptop and a notebook on the table, sipping on her pregnant lady glass of orange juice. Behind the booth table, her baby bump pushes against her red sweater. What is she now, five months along? Something like that?

"Grace." I collapse in the booth beside her, breathing hard.

"Oh my god. Grace."

The matchmaker places her glass down with a thump. She tucks her brown hair behind her ear, frowning at me with concern. "Nina? Are you—what's going on?"

Can't breathe. Can't speak. All I can do is shake my head and swallow hard, slapping my palm on the table. I'm too young to have a heart attack, right?

I mean, I know I eat too much take out. But I do kickboxing videos three times a week, and I feel strongly that those should count for something. Even when I get bored and lay down on the floor half way through.

"Easy." Grace waves at someone over my head, then shuffles up to make room. "Whatever it is, we'll deal with it. Okay?"

I jump as Grace's husband Aiden slides into the booth beside me. "Oh, shit! Jesus. You're like a big cat." A copper-haired mountain lion. My legs shake as I shuffle around the bench. "Why were you lurking over there?"

Aiden rolls his eyes, but it's Grace who answers with an airy wave. "He's playing bodyguard. Aiden here doesn't like it when I meet strange men for work, so he comes along and glowers in the background."

"Oh." I steal another glance at Grace's taciturn husband. Presumably he talks with her, but with everyone else, he's really not a chatterbox. Guess I wouldn't be either if my throat was messed up like his. Whenever he speaks, I fight a wince. "That's really nice."

Aiden's mouth twitches behind his beard, and he gives me a nod.

"So who are you meeting?" I ask Grace weakly, suddenly desperate to prolong this conversation. It's not that I don't want to tell her, but where do I even begin? How can I tell her that my boss, the man that Grace knows I'm head over heels in love with, confessed his attraction to me in a Soulmate Express message? To a woman that doesn't exist? My accidental catfish persona? How the hell do I untangle *that*?

"A guy named Cain. He works with Griff in Mountain Rescue, and he has a cabin way up on the mountain. Up in the sticks, you know? Cain saw his buddy being all smitten with Luna and decided he wanted to try for his own match."

Grace taps her pen on her notebook, reading over her notes. Distracting the matchmaker with her Soulmate Express work is always a surefire way to buy time. "Apparently he's huge. Like, sometimes hikers come down the mountain yelling that they saw Bigfoot. Griff says—"

The crowd swells all around our booth, the chatter getting louder and drowning out the faint sounds of country music drifting from the jukebox. Grace cuts herself off, leveling me a look.

"Stop messing with me. What's going on, Nina?"

I swallow hard. My throat is so dry.

"I'll give you two some space," Aiden mutters, getting ready to move, but I shake my head fast. It might help to get a male perspective, after all.

"No, wait. I got this—this message tonight. Look." My fingers are clumsy, fumbling my phone as I draw it out of my jacket pocket. The Soulmate app is already open on the screen, my message from MrWrite as clear as day.

Exhaling, I slide my phone onto the table. Grace and Aiden lean closer on either side, and I stare up at the ceiling, miserable and excited and so confused.

They take so freaking long to read the message. What are they, illiterate? I scowl and distract myself by watching the micro-expressions flitting across Aiden's chiseled face, then peek at the shocked, round eyes of his wife.

They're a beautiful couple, I'll give them that. If I weren't tangled up in an emotional pretzel over Merrick Bates, I'd think this was quite the sexy sandwich.

"Merrick sent you this." Grace sounds dazed, and I slap the table again with my palm. Correct! *Dazed* is the correct response.

"Yes. Or he sent it to SomethingsGottaGive, anyway. But I'm his only assistant. Who else could he..."

I trail off, suddenly queasy. There was that intern last year who helped Merrick research an article. At the time, he barely seemed to remember she existed day to day, but maybe...

"It's about you." Grace settles a soothing hand on my arm. On my other side, Aiden nods. "I promise, Nina. Don't let yourself doubt that. Merrick wants *you*." I open my mouth, but Grace is already leaning forward, talking directly to her husband. "See? I told you they were meant to be together! Another soulmate match in the bag. The perfect record lives on, baby."

Aiden huffs a laugh, shaking his head.

Ugh.

"Meanwhile, I'm right here."

"Sorry." Grace sits back, her smile sheepish. "And we are one hundred percent here for you, but I've gotta say, Nina, I'm surprised you're here talking to us instead of charging over to Merrick's cabin. Why are you wedged in this booth when you could be tearing off your hot boss's clothes?"

I open my mouth, then close it again.

An excellent question.

Could I really do that? Would Merrick want me to? What if

he prefers to keep it all in his head? What if he realizes that I have no idea what I'm doing? What happens then?

"I've never..." I pick at a scratch on the booth table. "You know, the whole seduction thing..."

Grace pats me on the head. It's both kind and annoying, especially when she says, "It's not really seduction when he desperately wants you, Nina. It's more like giving him the green light. No flair required."

I turn to Aiden for confirmation. "Really? Is that true?"

Slowly, he nods. "If he wants you, that's it," Aiden rumbles. God, that throat sounds painful. "Don't overthink it."

Hmm.

Don't overthink it.

What an alien idea.

"I could go over to his cabin," I say, testing the idea out loud, "and I could knock on Merrick's door, and I could tell him I want him. And it would probably work out fine."

"Better than fine!" Grace glances out at the crowd and sits up straighter, waving at a man working his way across the bar. He's a complete giant, easily standing head and shoulders above everyone else, and his dark eyes are cautious above his black beard. He looks between Aiden and I as he gets close.

"That's our cue," I mutter, following Aiden out of the booth. Grace's husband strides over to the bar, leaning with his arms folded where he can keep an eye on his wife. I turn and wave at the matchmaker as her next client arrives.

"Wish me luck."

"You don't need it," Grace says, right as the newcomer rumbles, "Good luck."

"Thanks." I beam up at Cain, the gentle giant looming over me in the bar, and resist the urge to punch him on his massive shoulder. "You too."

The crowd is a sweaty, seething mass, and by the time I fight my way back out onto the street, my cheeks are flushed and I'm breathing hard.

I should go home and change clothes. At least drag a comb through my hair.

Instead, I set off for Merrick's cabin.

Merrick

‿◦⟡◦‿

I scrub both palms down my face and tip back in my desk
chair with a groan. All around me, the cabin is dim, lit
only by firelight. I got caught up again, wrapped up in
my work, and now my neck is stiff and the sky is ink black
through the windows.

Hunger gnaws at my stomach, and my throat is dry. When
did I last eat? Or drink a glass of water? Why do I forget the
basics of human maintenance every time I sit down at this
desk?

It's this book. This goddamn book. Can't believe I ever
thought it was a good idea. Sure, it could launch me to the next
stage of my career, but all this process has *actually* done is trap
me in the wilderness with my gorgeous, off limits assistant.

Kind of hard to focus knowing that Nina is right there. It's
not like back in the city, where there are blocks and blocks
between us, a master plan required to get from one door to
the other. Here, she's a short walk away, cozied up in the
lodgings I rented for her. Maybe even bored and looking for

some entertainment, and if I swore to myself to keep things PG, maybe I could—

A knock interrupts my racing thoughts. Probably for the best.

"Merrick?" Nina's voice is muffled by the cabin door, but even like this, she sounds... off.

My legs are stiff as I shove to my feet, the chair clattering along the floorboards behind me. I stride across the cabin, pausing only to switch on a lamp, and golden light fills the room. Better.

When I pull the door open, Nina hovers on my deck. She's bundled up in a random assortment of clothes, like she dressed while blindfolded and in a hurry. There's a pair of green yoga pants; a white sweater with penguins on it, a purple running jacket, and on her feet, thick hiking socks crammed into sandals.

"Nina." Her black hair is windswept and wild, half scraped back in a messy bun, and it seems damp. A flush stains her tan throat. "Are you alright?" Taking her elbow, I draw her inside, peering out at the dark treeline before closing the door.

If someone is harassing her... if they followed her here...

I'll kill them. With my bare hands, I'll tear them limb from limb.

But Nina doesn't seem frightened as she pads further into my cabin. She's not checking the windows or asking me to call the cops, she's just... staring at me. Turning around in the center of the rug and blinking at me with those soulful eyes.

My stomach drops. "This is about earlier, isn't it? What I said on our walk—about everyone wanting you." My voice is pure gravel, and I clear my throat. "I made you uncomfortable."

Fuck.

This is everything I've feared for the last two years. Ever since I first laid eyes on Nina Perez, I've been walking a tightrope, forcing myself to stay balanced and not allow her to see the urges she brings out in me.

The primal instincts. The need to claim her, fuck her, *love* her.

Because yeah, that's a surefire way to a lawsuit—but more importantly, to making Nina feel unsafe at work.

"Forgive me." My chest is raw and aching. I rub a hand over my jaw, the bristles of my beard crackling softly. "I should never have spoken to you like that."

"No, I'm glad you did," Nina murmurs. She's plucking at the hem of her white knitted sweater, her gaze fixed on me. Is she nervous? She seems tense where she stands, like she's thrumming with an invisible tension. "I liked it, Merrick. I wish you'd say more things like that."

Uh. What's that now?

"I'm..."

Having a stroke?

"...Not sure that I follow. Why are you here, Nina?"

And why is she staring at me like that, plump lips parted, her eyes so beseeching? Why does she keep plucking at that sweater like she's thinking about pulling it off and showing me the perfect body hidden underneath?

What is *happening*? Did I fall asleep at my desk?

"Merrick." Nina huffs, and okay, this is familiar. Grounding, too. Exasperated Nina is a Nina I can handle. "Don't make me do all the work here. Either you want to kiss me too or you don't, but either way—"

I cross the cabin in three strides. My heart riots in my chest the whole way, my pulse thudding in my ears, and my hands shake as I cup the sides of her face. Can't believe what she just said.

"Want to kiss you too," I say, and if this is a dream, I won't fight it anymore. Why would I ever want to wake from this?

My head lowers, and Nina sucks in a sharp breath.

The world tilts as her mouth meets mine.

* * *

I've wanted to kiss Nina Perez every single day since I met her. I've thought about how she'd taste; how she'd sigh; the warmth of her body against mine. The silky slide of her black hair through my fingers, and the flutter of her eyelashes against her cheeks.

I've thought about tossing her up onto my desk and stepping between her spread thighs; daydreamed about flattening her against a wall.

I've thought about this non-stop, so really, there's no way that the reality should live up to the expectations.

It's Nina, though. So I shouldn't be surprised that the reality is *better.*

"God." I can't decide where to put my hands. Want to touch her everywhere all at once. Nina laughs weakly into our kiss as I grip her hips then squeeze her waist; as I trace my thumbs over the curve of her tits then slide my hands up to cup her throat. "God, Nina. Wanted you for so damn long."

Her breath hitches and her mouth slants harder against mine. Her kiss is unpracticed but so passionate, and that combination makes me harder than stone. I'm rigid in my jeans, blood throbbing in my shaft, and I want her, I want her, I *want* her.

Plunging my hands into Nina's hair, I tilt her head back and mouth kisses along her jaw. If there's a scrape of teeth... well, I'm feeling savage.

She's mine. This is happening.

"Merrick," Nina gasps, fumbling to hold onto my arms for balance. "Oh my god. Oh, wow."

Yeah.

This is a lot.

"You've wrecked me, Nina." My words are guttural, and when I catch her wrist, my grip is firm. I lower her hand between us, then press her palm against my aching bulge, her nails scratching over the denim. "Feel what you do to me, beautiful girl."

"Um." Slender fingers explore me greedily, but her eager hand is a direct contrast to her anxious expression. "It's—you feel—Merrick, I don't know what I'm doing."

I swallow hard, heart thudding. Did I go too far? "We can stop anytime."

"*No.*" Nina grips my cock harder through my jeans, and I choke out a shocked laugh. If a gale swept through this cabin, it's like she'd use my length as a handhold. "No, I don't want to stop. But I need some direction."

I hesitate.

My assistant scoffs, tossing her wild hair back. "Come on, Merrick. You're always so bossy."

Because I'm her literal boss—but fine. I'll let that one go.

"Move back," I tell her, walking her carefully across the cabin. Nina shuffles backward, clinging to my arms again, blinking up at me with so much trust. She lets me walk her all the way to my desk, then leans her ass against the edge of the wood and gazes up at me.

Papers crinkle behind her. Nina bites down on a grin. "You

know, if you kept a tidier desk, you could sit me on it—"

"Don't torment me."

Her soft laugh mingles with the pop and crackle of the fire.

We're slower, now. Kissing softly, our movements lazy, like we've both agreed that we're not stopping any time soon and so there's no reason to rush. The slide of Nina's tongue against mine—it's decadent.

I nip her bottom lip, breathing hard. Nina reaches between us and palms the hard bulge behind my jeans.

"So…" Her mouth quirks up, and she's so perfect that it hurts my stomach. "A little direction here…"

"Undo my jeans." I sound ruined. Like I've been yelling at top volume in a storm. And when Nina flicks my buttons open one by one, the pad of her thumb smoothing over the brass, a sudden headache squeezes my temples.

She's my assistant. There are rules for a reason. What the fuck am I doing?

"Don't need to do this," I grit out as her hand dips inside my clothes. Slender fingers wrap around my cock, and I hiss between my teeth. "Nina. You can change your mind."

Even as I say the words, I buck into her hold, sliding her hand along my length. She grips me loosely, working me over with a maddeningly light touch.

"Nina," I rasp, and I'm surprised my legs are holding out. Don't remember what I was about to tell her—to stop or to grip me harder? To pretend this never happened or to get on her knees and open wide? "Nina, this is—tell me you're okay. Tell me what you're thinking."

Our clothes rustle softly as she gains confidence. Gains speed. "I'm thinking about all the times I wanted to suck your cock, Merrick. All those times I wanted to crawl under the desk in your office and just go to town."

Ah, Jesus.

My head pounds, but I don't care. I thrust into her grip, wrapping my hand around her shy fingers. Coaxing her to hold me tighter.

"Would you like that, boss?" Nina grins up at me, eyes twinkling. She knows exactly what she's doing to me, the little demon.

"You know I fucking would." But I like her surprised gasp when I spin her around even better; I like kicking her feet apart and pressing her down with a hand spread between her shoulder blades. Nina melts beneath my touch, so eager, so willing.

I'm going to lick her pussy until she cries.

"Is this how you imagined it?" She's breathless and flushed, papers crinkling beneath her cheek. Her round ass wiggles and I choke back a curse, gripping myself at the root to keep in control. She's a sight to behold, hair mussed and clothes in disarray. Red-cheeked and panting, offering herself up to me. "When you imagined bending me over the furniture, is this how you pictured it?"

I pause, stomach clenching.

That is… a very specific question. And I didn't become a journalist by missing the buried clues, nor by ignoring the instincts screaming in my brain. Something is off.

"How do you know about that?"

She stiffens under my touch, and my voice hardens. "How do you know about that, Nina?"

Did she read my messages somehow? Did I log in to Soulmate Express on her work laptop, then forget? No, I'd never be so careless, and yet I've only ever admitted those thoughts about Nina to one single soul.

I step back, the cabin spinning around me. My gut churns as I tuck myself away, refastening my jeans before Nina turns around.

Off. Something is very off.

"You're SomethingsGottaGive." The pieces thunk into places, everything slotting into a hideous puzzle. Nina's hugging herself, and she looks as miserable as I feel. As she stares at me, tears brim in her eyes and I twitch forward, fighting the need to draw her against my chest.

No. I can't let myself weaken. I need answers first.

"You catfished me?"

She flinches and shakes her head. The flush on her throat darkens. "No, of course I didn't. Come on, Merrick. It was a genuine mistake, okay? When we were first matched, I had no idea."

Alright... fine.

I pinch the bridge of my nose, and I swear to god, I'd trade a year of my life for this headache to go away. It's squeezing my skull in a vice grip, making every crackle of the fire and rustle of Nina's clothes an assault on my senses.

"When did you realize?" I ask, already dreading her answer. Because what I really want to know is: how long did she lie to me for? How many days or weeks have passed with Nina carrying this secret around, while I blunder around in the dark like an idiot?

"Since the photo of your desk."

I close my eyes, swaying on my feet. That was weeks ago. She's known all this time? She knew and she didn't tell me?

Acid spreads through my gut. It burns me.

"I'm sorry," Nina says, but I can't listen. Can barely hear

anything over the roaring in my ears. "I wanted to tell you, okay? So many times. But I didn't think you'd want me, only your mail order match, and then I'd lose you *and* my job. I never wanted to lie to you, Merrick—"

"But you did." Anger pounds through my body, crackling in my veins, and I could tear this whole cabin apart board by board. "You did lie to me, Nina. God damn it."

"I'm sorry," she tries again, and I hate the desperation in her voice. Hate the guilt gnawing on my ribs, telling me *I'm* out of line here, when she's the one holding all the cards. I hate every single thing about this. "If we could just start over—"

"No." I cut her off, staring at the dark windowpane. At our reflections, warped in the firelight. I don't recognize either of us. "No, Nina. This was a mistake."

Her pained exhale—that breaks something inside me. And when she stumbles to the cabin door, I open my mouth to call her back.

No words come. The door slams shut, and the sound is so final.

Fuck.

What a night.

* * *

It's only once my blood has cooled and I've swallowed two painkillers to dull the ache in my head that I can finally think clearly again. I pace back and forth on the cabin rug, my stomach lurching with each step.

Did I do the right thing? Was I too harsh? Too hasty?

The memory of pained shock on Nina's face when I told her no...

I groan, tugging on my own hair. The wind rattles the windows, and shadows dance across the cabin floor.

She seemed so eager. So honest. Like she truly wanted my touch; like she was as thrilled by our kiss as I was. The way she smiled against my mouth—the way she slid her tongue against mine—

"Jesus." I pace faster, back and forth. Back and forth. I have a sickening sensation that maybe I got this wrong.

Does it matter that Nina knew and didn't tell me? What did she say—that she worried she'd lose her job?

That's fair. Of course that's fair. Not that I'd ever fire her over something like that, but it's reasonable that she'd worry about it.

I'm an asshole.

And… she canceled our mail order match right after the desk photo. As soon as she realized, she called it off.

"Nina," I mutter, and her name is bitter on my tongue. "God, Nina."

What exactly should she have done differently? She didn't make me declare that I wanted her. She never asked leading questions or used her anonymity against me. And the same night that I confessed everything to her by mistake, she charged right over here because she wanted me too. Dressed in those damn hiking socks and sandals—the girl who always takes such care with her clothes.

The ghost of her touch prickles over my cock. I'm still hard, my shaft an angry bulge in my jeans, and I deserve this. I deserve the worst case of blue balls in my life.

She put it all out there, and I punished her for it.

"Nina," I say again, and I guess it's the only word left in my vocabulary. It's certainly the only thought pounding in my brain. Every thump of my heart, every intake of breath, it's all I can think: *Nina. Nina. Nina.*

Gotta go. My girl's out there, hurt and upset, and I did that. I'm the goddamn elephant that trampled on her feelings.

Need to set things right. I wrench the cabin door open, the cold night air slapping my cheeks.

I'm coming, Nina.

Nina

⁓❦⁓

I toss an open suitcase on top of the navy bedspread, muttering under my breath. It's too late to catch a bus out of Cloudy Lake tonight, but I'm packing anyway. Going to get the hell out of here at dawn.

Merrick. The thought of my boss seizes the air in my lungs. I force myself to breathe through the radiating waves of pain and heartbreak, the anger and embarrassment. The fear.

Will he care that I'm gone? Or will he be relieved?

And what will I do now?

Guess I'll go back to the city. Find another job with another bossy jerk to perform miracles for. Or hey, maybe I could sign up for Soulmate Express and take another potshot at love.

Ha. Such bullshit. I toss an armful of clothes into my suitcase, not bothering to fold anything.

I'm surer than ever: love is the biggest con on earth. See, you can fall into it so sweetly, with nothing but good intentions. You can put yourself out there, risk your whole heart and soul on the line just like all the stories say you should, but what do you get in return?

A Merrick Bates-sized boot print, right on your heart. I sniffle, tossing a brush and hairdryer into the suitcase.

I can't even be that mad at him. That's the worst part. Merrick's right to be pissed off about the Soulmate Express messages; he's right to send me away. But I can't help thinking... how did we come to this? Two years, I've loved this man, and now I'm not sure he'll even write me a decent reference.

Ugh.

Rounding the bed to grab a stack of books off the dresser, I catch sight of myself in the mirror and take in my outfit with slow, anguished blinks. My penguin holiday sweater and green yoga pants? Hiking socks and sandals? I look like a kindergartner allowed to dress herself for the first time.

This is the outfit I wore to get rejected by the love of my life?

"Perfect." I drop the stack of books from chest height, glaring at the jumble in my suitcase. I hate everyone and everything. "Freaking perfect."

It doesn't take long to pack. These lodgings are comfortable but small, and I'm moving with furious efficiency. Tossing everything I brought here into the case with reckless abandon, grinding my teeth together the whole time.

Can't believe I did that.

Can't believe he wouldn't listen.

Can't believe any of this.

At first light, I'll drag this stupid case down to the bus station and get on the first bus that shows up. Don't care where it's going—I just need to get out of here, far, far away from Merrick Bates, and once I'm in another town, I'll be able to think clearly again. Plan a route out of the mountains and restart my life.

All that stuff.

The thought of Grace nudges at me, and I swallow around a lump in my throat. She'll understand, right? It's too late to go and find her tonight to say goodbye, but she'll get why I had to leave in a hurry.

Maybe she could visit me in the city. Or I could come back here, once I'm one hundred percent sure that Merrick's gone.

God. Staring out of the dark window at the high street below, watching the locals stroll past the streetlamps, bundled up against the cold, it hits me: I was building a life here. Making friends and getting comfy. Learning my favorite cafes and picking a favored machine in the launderette.

Because in the back of my mind... I hoped Merrick and I might stay here. Together.

Well, the joke's on me, and I yank open the last drawer of clothes, snatching up an armful of panties. I toss them over the bed, scraps of lace raining down like confetti, then stiffen as a knock rattles my door.

"Nina?"

I know that voice. It haunts my freaking dreams. My eyes dart to the window, but I'm two floors up.

"Nina? I know you're in there, sweetheart. I can see the light under the door."

Crap. Maybe I could knot the bed sheets together and dangle out of the window like a princess?

"Go away," I yell, twisting a pair of yellow lace panties in my hands. "Come back during office hours, Merrick." Sure, I'll be long gone by then, but he doesn't know that, does he?

A harsh laugh floats through the door. "And let you skip town? I don't think so."

Ah. Okay. So he does know me a little, but that doesn't

mean I owe him a conversation. Merrick said it himself—what happened between us was a mistake.

A breathtaking, agonizing mistake.

Every heartbeat is sore. I close my eyes briefly, safe in the knowledge that Merrick can't see this: my whole body stiff and trembling with hurt. Another knock on the door brings me back to reality, and I suck in a shaky breath.

"You can't make me open it, Merrick."

There's a long pause. And then: "I know."

I bite my lip, frowning at the door, because he doesn't sound pissed off anymore. He sounds exhausted and resigned and like he hates this distance between us as much as I do.

Wetting my lips, I risk asking: "Why are you here?"

Floorboards creak out in the hall. Merrick's voice comes closer, like he's speaking inches from the wood. "Because I fucked up, Nina. You didn't do anything wrong, and I let my temper chase you away. There's no excuse, but I was embarrassed and confused and I thought you were playing me—"

"I wasn't!"

"I know," Merrick says, his low voice so soothing through the wood. "Of course I know that. Fuck, I'm sorry Nina. You don't have to take me back, but please... let me make sure you're okay."

Um. Take him back?

So I really had him back there, for a moment?

Take him *back*?

Shuffling around the bed, I glance down and curse at my stupid socks and sandals. Life is cruel. I kick off the shoes at least, then toss the panties I'm strangling into the case before reaching for the door.

…Can I really do this? I pause with my hand on the doorknob.

It hurt so much when he didn't want me. Do I really want to open myself up to that again? To let the same man, this man I've loved for so long, break my heart twice? In this freaking penguin sweater?

"Please," Merrick says, low and desperate behind the door. "Please, sweetheart."

Ah, hell. I brace myself and swing the door open.

* * *

Merrick stalks into my lodgings, all piercing blue eyes and wind-mussed blond hair. The collars of his dark coat are turned up, the black points sharp against his beard, and god. The sexy gentleman lumberjack strikes again.

So unfair.

"Nina." My stomach muscles are tensed, my whole body bracing for an oncoming storm, but Merrick cradles my face so tenderly. His thumbs stroke my cheeks. "Fuck, Nina. I'm so sorry."

He looks broken as he swipes away the steady stream of tears that have been coursing from my eyes. For the record: I am not a pretty crier. I'm puffy and snotty and red-faced.

Don't know where to put my hands. I settle for tangling my fingers in his coat sleeves.

"Talk to me," Merrick murmurs, and every breath I take smells like him. Like pine and mint and fresh mountain air. It makes me want to sob and bury my face in his throat; makes me want to twist his hair until he yelps.

"What is there to say?" I shrug, giving a watery sniff. "You said it was a mistake. And you were right."

"No. No, Nina, I had it all wrong—"

"I mean, what did I think was going to happen?" It's too hard to keep looking in those intense blue eyes, so I fix on a spot on the wall over Merrick's shoulder. We haven't even mentioned this yet, but it's the elephant in the room, even if we can get past the rest of this mess. "That you were going to risk your big shot reputation to date your assistant? That you'd invite all that censure and gossip? Hardly."

Merrick steps closer and shakes me gently. "You're worth it, Nina. It would be worth it."

My eyes slam closed, and I draw in a shuddering breath.

He can't mean that. Sure, it's easy to say, but when the first bitchy comments from his rivals start to emerge, when it overshadows the release of his book, when an online horde with digital pitchforks try to cancel him—

"I mean it, Nina." Merrick places his mouth against my temple, his beard tickling me as he speaks. "Stop second guessing and overthinking. I'm in this, if you'll forgive me."

If I'll forgive him? For what? I mean yeah, he hurt my feelings back there, but his reaction was completely understandable. I'd probably have been way more irrational if the situations were reversed, and yet Merrick is here, knocking on my door and begging forgiveness.

Here's a groundbreaking thought: maybe my boss is not a jerk after all.

My fingers pluck at his coat sleeves. The fabric is chilled from the mountain wind, and his forearms are strong and sculpted beneath.

I barely got to see him earlier. You know: undressed and undone. I touched him briefly, but it wasn't enough.

Something tells me it will never be enough.

"I'm going to find another job." My words are uneven, and Merrick nods against my temple.

"Alright."

"You can't boss me around anymore."

He grins against my hair, and his voice drops so low that I shiver. "We'll see."

"And—and you have to delete your Soulmate Express profile."

"For fuck's sake, Nina," Merrick says, exasperated, but his hands are roaming down my shoulders as he talks. "I'm not going to date other women. I want *you*. 'Til death do us part, as they say."

Aah! Strong hands spread over my back, arching me against him. I blink up at my gorgeous, hungry-looking boss, and the room goes hazy.

This kiss is fierce. So harsh my head bows back. There's a desperate edge to it, an undercurrent of lingering fear after we nearly lost each other—after we nearly ruined this before we began. We swap silent stories of how much we hated it, how scared we were, communicating with bruising kisses and sharp teeth.

No more. We're both done being idiots, and if he's in, I'm in. I unbutton Merrick's coat and shirt as we kiss; I slide my palms over his warm, bare skin. His chest is strong, dusted with dark blond hair, and his nipples pebble in the cool night air.

Merrick groans as I rake his chest with my nails.

"You didn't even mention my outfit," I murmur against his lips. "That's how I know you're a good guy."

Merrick snorts, walking me back toward the bed. "Convincing evidence."

"Well, I would definitely have commented if you turned up here dressed like a sock puppet."

Merrick's grin is sharp as he reaches past and yanks the suitcase onto the floor. It thuds onto the rug, tossed panties tumbling everywhere. "Guess I'm a better person than you. Jesus, how many pairs of underwear do you own?"

"Hey." I grab his bristly chin and force his gaze back up to mine. It's razor sharp, his pupils blown wide. "Spoilers."

Strong hands grip my waist. There's a flash of a wicked smile. Then the room tilts and spins, and I'm laughing, loud and bright, as my asshole boss crawls on top of me.

Merrick

Where to begin? For a sickening stretch of time tonight, I thought I'd lost Nina. Thought I'd never again hear her throaty laugh or feel her fevered skin against mine. But she's here and I'm here and her arms have looped around my neck. Nina's tugging me closer, her legs parting around my waist.

"Beautiful girl." I nip her chin and press kisses along her jaw, then grind down against her, flattening her against the creaky mattress. "Your hand on me earlier—you don't know how insane that made me feel."

Nina splutters a laugh, tugging on two handfuls of my hair. "Oh, please. I had no idea what I was doing."

She doesn't need to know. Doesn't need to have fancy moves and techniques. It's enough that it's *her* arching beneath me, her gray eyes hazy.

I've thought about this so many times. Dreamed of pressing her thighs wide and sinking into her wet heat; imagined her whispering my name. Getting tangled up in Nina's long limbs and losing myself in her perfect body.

"Merrick?"

I shake my head, forcing myself to focus. "Yeah?"

"Oh, good. I thought you were taking a nap."

My growl makes her laugh, but my hips thrusting between her legs—that makes her moan.

Nina's still fully dressed. Still wearing that ridiculous outfit. It takes a herculean effort, but I drag myself back off her and stand at the foot of the bed.

"Strip," I command.

Nina's breath catches. Her fingers tremble as she sits up, reaching for the hem of her white sweater.

The penguins are the first to go. She's wearing a pink vest top beneath, and that sails over my shoulder, followed by two balled up hiking socks, thrown one by one. It's an odd striptease, I'll give her that, but with Nina's gray eyes fixed on mine, it's also the hottest thing I've ever seen.

"The yoga pants," I scrape out when she pauses, still in her pants and bra. "Take it all off, Nina. I won't ask again."

Her throat bobs as she swallows, and yeah. I knew she liked me bossy.

I wait until she's lifting her hips, wiggling her yoga pants and panties down in one go, before shrugging off my shirt and coat and letting them drop to the chaos on the floor.

Boots: off.

Clothes: gone.

My heartbeat is loud in my ears as I crawl back onto the bed, naked.

"We can stop anytime." Because sure, bossing Nina around is fun, but only if she's into it. "If you don't like anything we do, just say."

"No kidding." Nina yanks me down on top of her, her knees hitching around my sides. "Now get back in character, Merrick. Let's pretend I forgot to put a meeting in your calendar. Or even worse: let's pretend I forgot your dry cleaning."

Brat. Nina grins up at me, eyes twinkling, and fuck, I love her so much. I'm overstuffed with it, my chest so full that it aches, and when I reach between our bodies and find her slick, soft folds, I nearly die on the spot.

She really wants this.

She really wants *me.*

It's too much. More than a man could ever deserve, but I'm greedy for her so I'll take it. I'll take everything Nina's offering me, and I'll count myself lucky for every second.

"Want to taste you." I'm rocking between her thighs, my hard length rubbing up and down her slit, coating me in her slickness. "Want to feel you come on my tongue, Nina, but right now—"

"Do it." Fingernails sink into my shoulders, and Nina rolls her body against mine. "I can't wait either, Merrick. Do it. Hurry up. *Please.*"

Ah, shit. Hearing her beg… it snaps the final thread of my control. Turns me savage.

I notch myself against her and start pushing, teeth bared against her throat.

"Easy," I murmur when she whimpers, and I'm reminding myself too. This is Nina's first time, and I won't hurt her. I'll go slow—do this right. So even though my blood is pounding through my veins and my instincts are screaming for me to thrust, I ease off, sucking kisses down her throat.

She softens again. Cards her fingers through my hair.

161

Whimpers, breathes faster, rocks her hips. She's ready to keep going, but I wait until her mewls are truly desperate before I sink another inch deeper.

"Oh," Nina says, and the base of my spine is damp with sweat. I'm shuddering and taut above her, held in check only by my need not to rush. "Oh. Okay. That feels... Merrick, that feels...
"

She raises her thighs higher against my waist; wriggles her ass and sucks my cock in deeper. I screw my eyes shut, breathing hard. Every nerve ending in my body is singing out.

"Trying to go slow here, Nina."

My assistant huffs. "Really? Why? Come on, Mr Bates, whatever you can dish out, I can take it—"

Can't help myself. I thrust inside her, the force of my body driving Nina up the bed. She yelps and clutches my shoulders, but it's shock rather than pain—her cheeks are flushed and her mouth curves into a filthy smile. "That's more like it."

I pound into her again, my teeth clenched and a tendon standing out on my neck. I fuck my way deeper, all the way inside her, until our bodies are sealed tight and her flushed skin is damp against mine.

"Nina." I push up on my hands and stare at her stomach muscles shuddering between us. Further down, when I draw out slowly, my shaft is glistening and harder than rock. That sight—my cock buried between her thighs—it undoes me.

I press forward again, mouth dry, and watch myself disappear inside her, inch by inch. So hot and slick and perfect, strangling me with her tight grip. "*Fuck*, Nina."

"Uh-huh." She's breathless. Strained. "Keep going."

And god, I want to. Every atom in my body urges me to take her fast and hard, to pound her into a babbling, sweat-soaked puddle. But I can feel how tight she is, so tight I can feel her frantic pulse against my cock, and I won't hurt her on her first time. Not even if she begs.

I push in, then draw out. Move slowly, teeth clenched.

God damn it. If she so much as hiccups, I'm going to come inside her.

"Merrick." Nina bats at my shoulder, frowning up at me, her black hair splayed over the rumpled bedspread. "Stop holding back. I can take it, I swear."

And I'm sure she could, because this is Nina after all—she's a warrior, and feisty as hell. She could handle anything.

But I want more than her endurance. I want her moaning for me; crying out. I want her so well-fucked after this that she never has a second thought in her life, and I want her addicted to me and coming back for more.

There will be plenty of time to take her hard and fast. Plenty of opportunities to stake a claim, and fuck the brat right out of her. Tonight, though, I want her first time to be everything she deserves. I want her to own this. To take what she wants from it.

The mattress creaks as I tip to one side, pulling Nina on top of me with a startled squeak. Our bodies are still joined, my length wedged inside her, and Nina blinks down at me in surprise.

Her hair is wild. Her chest heaves. She looks like some kind of feral mountain woman, one who wandered down from the summit and claimed her man.

"You want it hard, sweetheart?" I grip her hips and squeeze. "Then ride me hard. Prove you can take it."

Nina

❦

I splutter, my nails digging into Merrick's strong chest. "Prove I can take it? Are you kidding me? This isn't a job interview, asshole."

But even as I berate him, I'm rolling my hips, gasping at the spark and crackle it sets off inside me. Digging my knees firmer into the mattress and shifting to find the perfect angle.

Oh, god. Every time I sink down on him, I'm so *full*.

Merrick smirks up at me, so smug and handsome and irritating as I rise and fall above him, settling into a steady rhythm. Broad hands grip my thighs, and blue eyes follow the soft bounce of my tits.

"Yeah, that's it. Just like that, Nina."

I sink my claws deeper. "I hate you."

Merrick chuckles. "No, you don't."

No, I don't. How could I hate him when his gaze on me is so hungry and reverent, the perfect mix of love and lust? How could I hate the thick slide of him inside my body, or the way that fine, okay, it's less sore when I'm on top? He's right, damn him. Always right.

I slam down harder, trying out different speeds and angles. Figuring out what I like—what makes my blood pound and my toes curl. He's just so solid and big and muscled, and I don't have to worry about squishing him or toppling him off the bed. He can handle whatever I throw at him, and I love that.

Turns out Merrick Bates is my favorite playground in the whole wide world.

"Feel this." Merrick catches my hips and rolls me toward him, keeping his cock deep inside. Sparks light up inside me, sweat beading on my hairline, and my breaths are ragged as I keep going, grinding down against him like I could corkscrew him down to the floorboards.

Holy. Shit.

His chest is flushed as I fold over it, still rocking and grinding. Merrick grabs two fistfuls of my hair, and sucks an angry kiss on my neck.

"You're going to come for me, Nina. Don't you dare stop now."

My thighs shake as I roll our bodies together. I'm so close—I'm *reaching*—

His breath is hot against my ear. "Good girl."

Those words slam into me, tightening my muscles and twisting my belly. They're a thunderclap, sending force waves rippling through my limbs.

And I sound wounded as I shudder and moan above Merrick; as my body clamps down on my boss's cock and my heartbeat booms in my ears. He's thick and hard. He's everywhere. So slick. So hot.

Oh. My. *God.*

I'm sweaty when I collapse down on his chest.

Don't care if I'm bright red. Too fuzzy.

"Nina," Merrick's growling, thrusting up into me below, already swelling inside me—then he stiffens too. Wet heat blooms in my core, and I grin against his collarbone.

Our breaths are ragged.

The room smells like sex.

Can't move. Can't move.

It takes a thousand years, but finally, I topple off Merrick to one side. He drags me close immediately, like I'm still a flight risk. As if. My legs are so wobbly, I'd never make it down the stairs.

"Can't believe I have to unpack again."

There's a brief pause, then Merrick says: "Well. You could unpack in my cabin."

Could I? *Should* I?

"No pressure," he adds quickly, "but as soon as you're ready, you should join me, Nina. God knows I want you closer. And besides, my cabin is nicer than this room."

I press my lips together, and I've never felt this light. Could float clean off the mattress and bob around the ceiling.

"Yeah," I say. "Tell me about it. My boss booked it, and he's a real asshole."

* * *

Six months later

"Oh my god." I wrench my hand from Merrick's grip, racing across the cobbled town square. My boots clatter against the stone, and the spring breeze ruffles my hair.

"Bye, then," he calls after me, but I'm deaf to my new husband.

I only have eyes, ears, and big goofy smiles for the plump baby cuddled in Grace's arms.

She stands with Aiden, chatting with some of our other friends from the mountain: Cain and Griff from mountain rescue, both bearded and burly, and Griff's silvery-haired wife Luna, tucked under his arm. They're all calm and steady, murmuring in low voices, and I arrive like a mini tornado.

"Oh my god. Grace. He's here! Baby Benjamin. You brought him out."

My friend turns to me, beaming with pride for her pudgy son. "I did! We're showing him around Cloudy Lake."

"Man, he's a real dumpling." I'm wheezing from my sprint, but I can't stop grinning. When I hold out one finger, a baby fist grabs hold, and Benjamin blinks up at me, a glob of drool streaking down his chin.

"I know, right?" Grace rubs the tip of her nose on his blue beanie. "So cute. Under here, he's got Aiden's copper hair."

"Very cute," I agree. And sticky.

Merrick joins us, more calm and dignified than I will ever be, and the men drift a few feet away to talk about trucks or sports or some other boring shit. All except one: huge, monstrous Cain with his black beard and kind eyes shuffles closer, bending at the waist to get a good look at the baby.

"Want to hold him?" Grace offers.

Cain blinks, clearly startled. "Can I?" he rumbles, his voice deeper than the mountain's ravines.

Grace beams happily and lifts Benjamin over. When the mountain man straightens, the baby clutched to his massive chest, I wait for Benjamin to howl for his mom, but he snuffles into the flannel shirt happily. A scarred hand settles over his back, and the two of them rock from side to side.

"Think the air's thinner up there?" I ask.

Cain rolls his eyes, but his beard shifts as he smiles. So good-natured. It sucks watching this man wait and hope for love, signed up to Soulmate Express for months now but never getting any takers. If life was fair, there'd be lines around the block for our local Bigfoot.

"It'll happen, Cain," Luna says softly, and Grace and I both nod. It has to, right? It *will.*

"Hope so," he mutters, stealing a glance at the nearby men, his ruddy face flushing darker. "I, uh. I tried something new. Put an ad in the personals."

"Going retro, huh?" We're all nodding. Smiling. Hoping. "Well, we're rooting for you, Cain. But you know what? I think you'll meet someone when you least expect it." Benjamin hiccups. "See? Even the baby agrees."

Twenty minutes later, I'm strolling hand in hand with Merrick again, and I can't get over the way Benjamin held my finger with his pudgy fist back there. My knuckle is still tingling.

My husband smells like mint when I lean in. "Hey, Merrick? Guess what. I want one of those."

"Your very own sasquatch?"

I barge his shoulder, but he stays steady, chuckling. Piercing blue eyes turn to me, appraising. "You want a baby, huh, Nina?"

"Yup." See, Merrick acts all calm and dignified, but *I* know how to read his handsome face. I can see the excitement brewing behind those eyes, and it makes my chest glow hot with happiness. This is a conversation I've already won. Maybe one that Merrick's been waiting for patiently. "I'll take it for walks, I swear."

His snort echoes down the sidewalk. Then Merrick's hand

tightens on mine, and he changes direction, towing me away from town back toward our cabin. My steps quicken too, until we're both breathless and laughing, marching home to our bed.

Our bed.

Our sofa.

Our shower.

Our kitchen table.

Whatever it takes, you know? Just ask my husband: I've always been a hard worker.

IV

Big Ol' Beard

Description

I'm studying birds in the mountains for the summer.
Then I discover Bigfoot.

Okay, okay, so he's not really a sasquatch—he's just a mountainous man in flannel. And sure, I shouldn't have screamed like that, but the guy took me by surprise, you know?

Because he's *huge.* So big and burly and bearded that in the fading light, I mistook him for a bear.

I think I really hurt his feelings, though. Our encounter haunts me—and when I figure out which one is his cabin, I can't help knocking on his door.

He thinks I'm being polite. And yeah, it started that way, but once I get a good look at him...

Oh, boy. I want so much more.

Abigail

⌘

I adjust my hold on the binoculars and squint against the fading light. The mountainside is quiet—the only sounds this evening are the whispering breeze, the rhythmic thudding of a beak against bark, and my own breaths.

"Oh, yeah," I murmur, inching forward. "There you are. Come to mama."

The carpet of pine needles softens my steps. A small shape moves between the branches overhead.

Honestly, I'm glad no one's around to see me like this. I'm dorky enough when I'm doing normal stuff, picking up groceries and putting gas in my truck. Swinging by the library and grabbing a take-out coffee in Cloudy Lake. But every time I catch a glimpse of my favorite species of woodpecker, I lose my shit. All dignity: gone.

That's why I work better alone. Turns out even scientists can be catty as hell, and who needs that?

Birds are much better.

"You're a big fella, aren't you?" The shape stops drumming

for a second, the silence extra loud before he starts up again. Shadows are stretching across the rocky floor, and the temperature's dropping. I've stayed out too long, I know I have, but I tramped around for hours looking for this guy.

I *just* found him. Can't leave yet.

The woodpecker is barely more than a patch of darkness against the tree trunk, his little head drumming against the bark, but in bright sunshine, he'd be striking: black and white and speckled, with a crimson quiff. It's late for him too, and I wonder idly whether he's struggling to find food.

My own stomach rumbles. I ignore it.

Holding the binoculars in one hand, I fish out my phone with the other and set it to record a voice note. Eyes glued on the shadow overhead, I whisper all the details I can come up with: sex, maturity, size, behavior, environment. The type of tree he's in. The dying light. I whisper into my phone while he drums at the tree trunk, and for a perfect moment, I'm completely at peace.

This is my purpose. This is what I'm meant to do: study woodpeckers far, far away from other people. And that pinch of loneliness I get sometimes, that yawning chasm in my chest—it's totally manageable so long as I get moments like these.

This red-naped sapsucker is all the company I need. *Right, buddy?*

A twig snaps nearby.

I pause.

My binoculars lower slowly, left to dangle against my chest on their strap, and I slide my emergency can of bear spray off my belt. My heart's drumming in time with the woodpecker. I definitely heard something. Definitely.

This whole summer, I've been alone in the mountains, and I've never used my bear spray once—but I feel a whole lot better with my finger on the nozzle. I turn slowly, my boot heel grinding into the dirt, the can raised in midair.

"Hello?" My voice quavers as I call between the trees, and I hate that. Hate how scared I sound. Because I am a scientist, damn it, and I am prepared for all eventualities. Whatever is out there, I can handle it.

But jeez, why did I stay out alone while it gets dark? Rookie mistake. Amateur hour. A bug bites my thigh, the pain hot and sharp, and I slap at my leg with my phone.

"Hello?" I call again.

The trees are silent. *Thud-thud-thud* goes the beak overhead, and *thud-thud-thud* goes my heart.

Okay, well. Mistake number one: staying on the mountain alone as it gets dark. Mistake number two: getting hooked on true crime podcasts over the summer. I've listened to way too many grisly accounts of murders in the wilderness, and now I'm paying the price for my morbid curiosity. I've spooked myself.

My palms are sweaty. I swallow hard.

Would bear spray work on people? It must, right?

Time to go. Sorry, mister woodpecker, but our time together is over. I shrug off my backpack, eyes still glued on the spaces between trees, and shove my binoculars away with shaking hands, tugging up the zipper. Then I slide my phone into the mesh pocket on the side, leaving the voice note recording just in case.

The homicide detectives will be so impressed with me.

As I straighten up, swinging my bag onto my shoulders, I keep the bear spray gripped so tight that my thumb aches.

Paranoia. That's all this is. I'll get back to my cabin and tuck myself away in the warmth and firelight and laugh at myself.

If I had friends, maybe I'd call and tell them this story too. See, the woodpecker's still drumming away, and if there really *was* something out here creeping up on me—

I turn to leave and slam into a huge shadow. As I bounce backward, arms flailing, bear spray bursts from the can. It arcs into the crisp evening air, and the creature roars so loud that the ground trembles.

I scream, landing hard on my ass, and scramble back across the dirt.

"Fuck!" the bear says, heaving and coughing overhead. It scrubs a very human arm across its eyes. "Jesus!"

The woodpecker flaps away, irritated. Fuck, indeed.

"I'm so sorry." My legs wobble as I push to my feet, and I shove the spray back onto my belt like it burns my hands. The air's thick with it, and my eyes are brimming too, wetness coursing down my cheeks, but *I* didn't get the worst of it. I didn't hit the stranger square on, but it all went in his direction. "Oh my god. I'm so sorry! I thought you were a bear."

The man—because obviously he's a man, even if he's the biggest human I've ever seen—coughs loudly, thumping on his chest. I wince, reaching toward him, then snatch my hand back.

What am I gonna do? Pat him on the shoulder and say "There, there"?

And besides. If he *is* a serial killer, this is all self defense anyway.

"Why were you right behind me?" I ask weakly.

"I'm with mountain rescue," the man grates between coughs. "Passing by. Came to see if you're lost. Fuck, let's move over

178

here."

Ah.

Okay, I am definitely the villain of this tale. I swipe my runny nose with the back of my hand, then trail after him to a patch of cleaner air.

What is the social protocol here? I've never accidentally assaulted a person before.

"Can I help you get home?" I offer.

The man rumbles a bitter laugh, before breaking into another round of coughing. "No," he wheezes at last. "I'm good."

Is he?

I frown at him through the gloom. Shoot, it really is dark. The first stars are winking overhead between the branches, and I can barely make out the shape of this guy. He's obviously tall and broad and bulky, and I think—I *think*—he has a beard. But that's all I'm getting from these streaming eyes.

"I'd really like to make sure you get home okay."

He sniffs hard and shakes his head. "No need. You get on inside so I don't need to worry about you."

He would worry about *me*? I've attacked some guardian angel of the mountain. So not cool.

"I'll go home right now," I promise quickly. "I'll go straight there, I swear. My cabin is a fifteen minute hike, tops."

The man's breaths rasp in and out of his chest. God, that sounds sore. "Alright," he rumbles at last. "Let's go."

Um. He wants to walk with me?

Why?

"I'm actually very good at orienteering. You don't need to worry about me getting lost. And, uh. I have plenty more bear spray."

The man puffs out a pained laugh, but when I turn to go, he falls into step by my side. "There are wolves in this area," he mutters when I glance up at his shadowed face. "Can't spray a whole pack of 'em, can you?"

Nope. Probably not. And if this man was a serial killer, he could have snapped my scrawny neck a dozen times by now. Jeez, just look at the size of him. My neck aches from looking up at him.

"I will never stay out past sundown again," I vow to my newfound protector. Lord, I've caused this man so much trouble. "I got distracted by this bird, but—"

"A bird?"

I beam, my steps getting bouncy despite the disastrous evening. "Yeah. A red-naped sapsucker."

The man grunts. "Sounds fancy."

"They *look* fancy, and they're just the best critters to watch. They drum at the tree bark, you know, drilling holes with their beaks, and then they drink the sap and eat ants…"

I trail off, blinking hard at the dark ground.

He doesn't want to hear this. No one ever wants to hear this.

But: "Go on," the man says after a pause, and his deep voice makes my insides tingle. I suck in a happy breath.

"Well, if you really want to hear it…"

It's strange, walking with this shadowed giant. Falling into step easily, because he must have slowed down to match me; talking his ear off about my favorite birds. First I thought he was a bear, then that he might murder me, but now I'm so, so comfortable with him. More at ease than I've ever been with another human being in my whole life. It's like we've magically fallen into sync.

Does he really like hearing about birds?

And he doesn't find me off-putting?

It's such a shame that I sprayed him with vicious chemicals. What are the chances he'd want to chat with me again? I chew on my bottom lip as we get closer to my cabin, and at last I can't put it off any longer.

"My name's Abigail. What's yours?"

"Cain," my would-be bear grunts.

Cain from mountain rescue. There can't be tons of those, can there? And I'm building up to something audacious, to something I've never, ever done, trying to find the words to invite this man inside my cabin for a hot drink. I'd give anything to see him in the light.

But when we reach my cabin steps, Cain hangs back in the darkness.

"Aren't you coming inside?" I blurt, asking him all wrong. Like I expected it or something weird.

Cain's massive shoulders shrug. "Better not. My face is all messed up."

I don't mind—god, how could I mind? I'm the one who sprayed him—but when I open my mouth to invite him inside anyway, to suggest he wash his face in my sink, Cain's already striding away.

No word of goodbye.

"Goodnight!" I call. "And sorry again!"

The shadow raises a hand, then melts back between the trees. I hover beside the cabin steps, my stomach tight.

Not my best social interaction, that's for sure. Not my worst, but far from my best.

Cain from mountain rescue. I grip the wooden rail and climb the steps, sniffing hard.

Really wish he'd come inside.

Cain

"God damn." Griff whistles low and long, staring at me in the doorway from his seat at the main desk. The mountain rescue headquarters are small, the main room crooked and cluttered, and the space feels full even before you add two bulky, bearded men. He winces at my red, itchy eyes. "Allergies?"

I sniff hard, pushing the door open wider. My head ducks automatically, my shoulders brushing each side of the frame as I squeeze myself inside, and I collapse onto the squashy sofa in a chorus of springs. "Nope. Bear spray."

"Shit." Griff drops his pen onto his desk. It clatters against the wood, then rolls and plunks onto the floor. Our fearless leader is hunkered behind the table, three stacks of paperwork penning him against the wall, but his eyes narrow. "If some fucker attacked you, Cain—"

Yeah, it wouldn't be the first time. Something about out-growing most men by a foot by the age of fourteen has painted a target on my back, and occasionally some idiot will drink too much and decide it's time for a challenge.

Never works, obviously.

But I'm already shaking my head. Whatever Abigail was last night, she was no *fucker*. "It was an accident. S'fine."

Aren't you coming inside?

She had a sweet voice. Light and fresh, like the mountain breeze. Would she have made me a drink?

Why didn't I go in?

Griff bristles, his chest puffing up under his gray shirt. The man's intense about outdoor safety—no room for messing around. The strict headmaster of the mountain. Guess that's why he's the boss, sitting at the nicer desk with fewer scratches, and mine's shoved against the back wall by the ancient radiator. Each October when the heating turns on, I cook one side of my leg.

Me, I prefer to give folks the benefit of the doubt. To forgive and forget.

Though with Abigail, forgiving was easy. Took less than five minutes. Forgetting, on the other hand...

"You look like hell, Cain." Griff's chair clatters against the wall, and he stomps to a bank of lockers. The metal drawers rattle as he digs for our first aid kit, and I watch my oldest friend in silence.

He's fussing over me, and it's nice that he cares. But let's be honest: I look like hell most days. Else why'd I get nailed with bear spray in the first place? There's a reason my local nickname is Bigfoot, that's all I'm saying.

Abigail didn't do any real harm.

Wonder if I'll ever see her again.

Would I recognize her if I walked past her in the grocery store? If we brushed elbows at the Cloudy Lake bar? I only saw her from the back before she got me with that bear spray, and after that I could barely make out the shapes of the trees. But if I heard her speak...

Yeah, I'd know her. From a hundred paces, I'd recognize her then.

"Cain?" Griff says, and it's clear he's said my name a few times already. He's pulled a chair next to the sofa, the first aid kit sprawled open at his feet, and there's a wipe in his hand and a bottle of eye drops in the other. "You ready?"

The sofa creaks as I shrug. "Sure." Ain't been fussed over like this since I was a boy, but it's fine by me. If playing mother hen will make Griff feel better, he can go right ahead.

I bet his wife Luna fusses him like this. Cleans his cuts and mops his fevered brow. Sounds like heaven.

Not when Griff does it, though. No offense to the man, because he's a good guy and my closest friend, but his big, scarred hands and dark beard aren't what I dream of hovering over me.

I want slender hands. Soft skin. Curves I can reach out and squeeze; a bright peal of laughter as I yank my helper onto my lap.

Bet Abigail's a caring woman. And I bet if I'd gone inside, she would've taken a look at my eyes too; maybe wiped them down with a damp cloth or something.

Seriously. Why didn't I go in?

"You want to check your messages?" Griff asks, frowning as he drops fluid in my eyes. I stare up at the ceiling, vision blurring from the drops.

He's not talking about work messages. He's talking about Soulmate Express. Shouldn't really check my mail order match profile during a shift, but I don't have internet in my cabin and

Griff's a laid back boss. He knows it's important to me. How badly I want what he has.

Love. A good woman. A family.

Someone to look after, and to be cared for in turn.

And normally I'd leap at the chance to log on, to see if I've had any interest over the last week, but this morning…

"I'm good."

Aren't you coming inside?

Maybe mail order matches aren't for me. Maybe I'll meet my woman the flesh and blood way. Hey, anything's possible— even for the local Bigfoot, right?

And since hearing Abigail's voice, since walking her home in the darkness, the thought of checking Soulmate Express… it just feels wrong. Maybe I'll get the matchmaker to delete my profile.

"You ever heard of a red-naped sapsucker?" I ask.

There's a long pause, and I can tell what my boss is thinking. He's thinking that maybe the bear spray addled my brains, and he should get me to count backward from one hundred. He's probably thinking that if I've gone nuts, if I've finally snapped, it'll take dozens of strong men to take me down. Maybe helicopters too, King Kong style.

"It's a bird."

Griff exhales and plops another eye drop in my eye. "Right. No, but there's a field guide on the shelf in the corner. Knock yourself out."

I will.

I settle back against the sofa, blinking hard.

I'll look up that little bird and find a picture of what Abigail was chattering about last night. Just as soon as I can see again.

* * *

Luna comes in with her friends at lunchtime, the open door letting in a fresh breeze. The three of them—Luna and Grace and Nina—they're a whirlwind of laughter and giggling, all cramming between the ancient furniture. The copper-haired baby Benjamin is cradled against Grace's shoulder, a dark patch of drool seeping into the matchmaker's green sweater, and she brings him straight over to see me at my desk.

"Hey, Cain. Benjamin here was wondering—oh crap, what happened to your eyes?"

When I reach out a single finger across the desk, her son grabs it and squeezes as hard as he can. It's not very hard. Like his dad, he's all bark but no bite.

Looking at the baby, my throat hurts. Must be the bear spray, so I tell Grace about last night, my voice rasping painfully.

Yeah, I'm still sore from all the coughing. That's it.

"I can't believe she did that to you!" Grace is puffed up and furious once she's heard, just like my boss was, and I appreciate that care well enough, but I wish they'd all lay off Abigail. They weren't there. It wasn't like that.

She didn't leap out at me screaming or some shit. I spooked her, plain and simple.

"She didn't mean any harm." I drop my voice, glancing past Grace's shoulder at the others. They're all chatting and laughing, Luna balanced on Griff's lap and trying to feed him a carrot stick. Nina's telling a story, throwing her arms around, her voice getting louder as she nears the punchline. "She, uh. When I walked Abigail home, she invited me into her cabin."

Can't look at Grace, though I desperately want to see her reaction. I stare at a box of bronze paper clips on my desk instead. Because as a Soulmate Express matchmaker, Grace knows love better than anyone else, and she'll understand whether I should've gone inside last night after all. If I missed my chance without realizing it.

"And once you were inside?" Grace prompts.

Ah, shit.

I prod the paper clips, my stomach tight. You know, I rescue folks from rock slips and mountain storms every month, and here I am feeling like the world's biggest coward.

"Oh, *Cain*," Grace says. Benjamin tugs on a lock of her brown hair, and she jiggles him higher against her shoulder. "Did you like her?"

Did I like her? Bear spray aside… yeah. I liked Abigail a whole lot. I liked the bouncy way she walked when she got excited, telling me all about her favorite birds. I liked the fact that she had a canister of bear spray on her belt, even though she nailed me with it—because she was prepared. A smart woman ready for the wilderness.

I liked the way she tried to walk me home, and that she asked for my name, and the disappointed way she said, *"Aren't you coming inside?"* Like she really wanted me there.

I liked everything about her.

Fuck. "Yeah." I peer up at Grace through sore, itchy eyes. She's pressing a kiss on her son's head, but her eyebrows are pinched in a frown. "Did I ruin it?"

Her mouth twists. Thought so.

Change of subject time. Can't stand any more pity, not when my belly is a pit of snakes.

Abigail. Can't believe I had a chance with her and I blew it.

"So what did Benjamin want to ask me?" I focus on his sticky, chubby face; his big, owlish eyes; the peaceful way he slumps against his mom's shoulder, sucking on a fist. This boy is happy in the knowledge that he's too young to be a screw up.

Lucky gnat.

"Oh, yeah. Barbecue at ours this Saturday? While the weather's still good."

We chat a while longer, making plans and small talk. I try to focus on what Grace is saying, and remind myself to be grateful. I'm lucky to be surrounded by such good people.

But when the ladies have gone and it's just me and Griff again, filling out paperwork and order forms in silence, waiting for the phone to ring with a cry for help—I can't help the ache in my chest.

When my boss raises a hand to scratch his beard, his wedding band glints under the ceiling light. *That.* I want that so badly.

With a certain birdwatcher, now I've met her.

God damn it.

Abigail

I knock softly at first, my knuckles gentle against the wood, but when the silence stretches on, I knock again a second time, harder. The force rattles the cabin door, the sound echoing around the clearing, and I scuttle back, suddenly nervous.

The deck creaks under my steps. The nearby trees rustle in the wind. The sky above is parchment white, the mountainside damp from rain showers all afternoon, and this cabin is wilder than the one I've rented for the summer.

The wood is older, the windows dark, and there are no plant pots on the sills or hum of a generator. This is wilderness, alright. Back to basics.

I shift my weight from foot to foot. Rehearse my speech again in my head.

Hi, Cain. It's me, your bear spray assailant. Just wanted to check that you're definitely okay, and that I haven't ruined your eyes for life. Oh, and please don't sue me. Ornithologists are not well paid.

Nope. That's not gonna do it, but I don't have time to come

up with something better, because the cabin door swings open and an enormous man ducks down to fill the frame.

Jeez. No wonder I mistook this man for a grizzly in the dark—he's *huge.* I feel like a pebble next to a boulder.

"Um." My voice cracks and I clear my throat. Cain ducks all the way out, coming to stand on his deck with his tree-trunk arms crossed. With his short dark hair and beard, tattoos winding around his forearms beneath his rolled shirtsleeves, he's not how I imagined he'd be.

Judging by his voice and his manners, I figured he'd be kindly and buttoned up. *This* Cain looks like he rode a motorbike up the mountain—one that was specially made for his bulk.

He looks down at me, perplexed, dark eyes watching me from his tan, weathered face. How old is this guy? Forty? There are speckles of silver in his black beard.

"Hi. It's—um. It's me."

He straightens as I talk, his thick eyebrows bouncing up. "Abigail," he rumbles. Like he's surprised to see me here.

That's fair. Cain didn't tell me where he lived last night, and it took me less than twenty four hours to track him down. That's creep behavior, let's be honest.

I raise my clammy palms. "I'm not trying to be weird. And I'll leave if you want, but I wanted to make sure you're okay." My shoulders tense as I peer up into his eyes—his red-rimmed, clearly sore eyes. "Oh. Ouch."

God. I am the worst person on this mountain.

Cain grimaces, scratching the side of his jaw. "It's not as bad as it looks."

"Really? Because it looks awful," I blurt, then cringe when Cain frowns at the deck. The blush crawling up my neck is red-hot. "Not that—*you* don't look awful, obviously, I just mean—"

"You need something, Abigail?"

Oh, I know that tone. That low level exhaustion, that world weary sigh that says I am a whole lot to deal with. I know it by heart. And surely no one in the world has as much right to be annoyed with me as this man, but the pained surprise still takes my breath away.

I thought... last night, I thought...

Well. That we were getting along. And sure, Cain didn't come inside when I invited him, but that could have been for loads of reasons. Like maybe he needed to walk home before it got too dark, or maybe he was hungry or tired.

Nope. I'm just hard work.

My arms wrap around my ribs, squeezing tight. Cain follows the movement, dark eyes steady, before his gaze flicks back to mine. A sad little zing shoots up my spine as he takes in my padded green jacket and backpack straps, my auburn hair pulled half-up to bare the tops of my ears, gone pink in the cold.

What, do I think that means something? Come on. "Sorry. No, I don't need anything. I'll go."

Why did I ever think coming here was a good idea? I blasted this poor man with freaking bear spray. Of course he never wants to see me again; of course this is a terrible surprise. If the roles were reversed and he nearly blinded me in the woods, I'd be running him off my property with a wood ax right now.

"Wait." Cain's voice is so deep, the vibration hums inside my bones. He jerks his chin at the cabin door. "Come and see something first."

...Hmm.

I chew on my bottom lip, still dancing from foot to foot. Go inside a strange man's cabin all alone, or offend the innocent man I attacked last night? I mean, I'm the one who knocked on his door.

Cain's tone is amused. "We can leave the front door open if you like. But I won't try anything, Abigail. I'm still recovering from our last encounter."

Crap. Okay.

"I have a pocket knife and a heavy flashlight in my bag," I warn him as I inch past. "And a fresh can of bear spray on my belt. And I'm scrappy."

His laugh breaks into a wheezing cough. "I bet you are," he rasps, following me inside. And now I feel idiotic, because Cain keeps a respectful distance, never coming closer than five feet, even though his cabin isn't huge. It's all one room except for what looks like a small bathroom, with the furniture gathered around a log burner in the center of the floor. A double bed is pushed against the far wall.

There's a faded red sofa and a coffee table and patterned rugs. A whittling knife on a scrubbed table, next to a lump of wood and a small pile of curly shavings.

I blink around, bemused, because it's so much more welcoming when you get inside. It feels like a real home. Like somewhere you could come after a long day of hiking or working or, say, bird watching, and collapse with a blissful sigh. Ready to be lulled by dancing firelight and the pop and crackle of burning wood.

"Here." Cain skirts around me, crossing to a bookshelf by the wall, and that careful distance makes my chest pinch. I'm the one who warned him off, but now that we're inside and I'm clearly safe, I hate the way he's orbiting me. Keeping out of reach. "I looked up that bird you told me about."

I perk up. "The red-naped sapsucker?"

Cain shows me a field guide, held open to the right page. "That's the fella. Is this him?"

It's an old book, well out of date, but the illustration is good. I beam at the mountain man, forgetting our awkward truce, and hurry closer.

"Yep. See that red patch on his head?" When I stop, we're close enough that I can feel Cain's body heat against my side. He smells like soap and sawdust and spice, and his knuckles are blunt where he holds the book splayed open. I tap at the page, the book wobbling slightly in his grip. "And the black and white plumage?"

"Sure."

"You wouldn't have seen it last night, but he'd have been a real beauty in the daylight." My eyes narrow as I scan the page. "This map's no good, though. The populations have moved quite a bit. May I?"

Cain grunts as I pluck the book from his hand, wandering over to a cup of pens and pencils on the bookcase. I choose a sharp pencil and set the book down, shading in a more accurate population spread.

"This is what I'm studying this summer." He didn't ask, but I can't seem to stop talking around this man. Mostly, I clam up around other people, not willing to get my emotional ass kicked, but some part of me must have decided to trust Cain implicitly, because I keep blurting out all kinds of nonsense around him. Poor guy. "The woodpeckers in this area, and how they're adapting to changes over time. I got a special grant."

"Sounds interesting."

I shoot a look at him, but he doesn't seem sarcastic. The

bearded giant has backed up and now he's leaning against the wall, arms folded, watching me. "It is," I agree, cautious. "It's exactly what I wanted to study when I was a little girl."

"But for now, you're only here for the summer."

I wet my bottom lip, my heart tapping against my ribs, and I have no idea why I'm so nervous all of a sudden. My pencil hovers above the page. "Well. If there's potential for long term study here, I could apply for another grant or a local conversation role. I could... I could stay."

And then it's happening: I'm getting that vertigo feeling, that sensation of the patterned rug rushing towards me as I realize we're having two separate conversations at the same time. One outright, and one hidden. God, I hate moments like these.

Am I messing this up? What am I *saying*?

"I'm sorry about your eyes," I say, suddenly desperate to get back on solid ground. "I can't believe I sprayed you like that. I'm such a dolt."

"No, you're not." Cain scratches his beard, glancing at my shaded map, then back up. "You're very smart, Abigail."

Yeah. Yeah, I am, in some specific ways.

And in other ways, I'm like a toddler blundering into pieces of furniture.

For instance: did Cain just want to show me this book, and now he's waiting for me to leave? Or was he hoping that I'd linger? And did that conversation mean he wants me to stay on the mountain longer than the summer? If I did, would it be okay if I visited him sometimes?

I would really love that. Even twisted up in anxious knots like right now, I love being near him. He's so steady, and his eyes are all crinkly at the edges from smiling. He was nice about my map, too. And he smells really good.

Is this man too old for me? Am I a pervert? What's that rule again—is it double your age minus seven?

"It'll get dark soon." Cain interrupts my mental arithmetic, nodding at the open door, and I glance outside at the gathering shadows. Oh, yeah. The outside world still exists. "You promised me you wouldn't get caught out after sundown again, Abigail."

So I did. "Scout's honor." I place his field guide down, drawing an imaginary cross over my heart. "I'll go now, then. Um. Sorry to bother you."

"You didn't." Cain follows me to the door, still keeping that careful distance. Damn me and my threats of bear spray. "Maybe I'll see you around Cloudy Lake, then."

I turn around on his deck and bounce on my toes. "Yeah, maybe."

We both pause, like we're waiting for something... but whatever it is, it never comes. We're hovering and awkward, and then the moment has passed.

"Okay." I lift one hand in a goofy salute, my stomach sinking. "Bye, then."

The wet ground seeps through my hiking boots as I tramp back to my rented cabin, dampening my socks and icing my toes, and the temperature drops as the sun sinks below the horizon. The trees darken, their branches black against the gloomy sky.

Dusk falls as I push open my front door, stamping the fallen leaves and clumps of dirt from my boots before I go inside.

It's a fancier cabin, one with electric light and a box heater, but it's nothing like Cain's cabin.

That one felt like home.

Cain

⁂

If there's one time in life when a man should concentrate, it's when he's dangling over a rock face by a rope. All manner of shit could go wrong, especially when you're what your boss sometimes calls 'jumbo sized' and the rope looks thinner than dental floss—but here I am daydreaming about the way Abigail's delicate ears turned pink from the cold.

You'd think I'd know better. I've scraped enough climbers and hikers and tourists off these rocks over the years, but here I am ready to break into song like some hairy Disney princess. I'm barely looking at where I'm putting my hands.

She came to see me yesterday. And she did, she *saw* me—in all my Bigfoot glory, out in the light. But Abigail didn't run screaming or burst out laughing, and she came inside my cabin after some coaxing. She trusted me enough to come look at my new book.

Did she like the bird illustration? Did she like the cabin? Did she like *me*?

Fuck, she was pretty. Small and soft and kinda birdlike herself. Wish Abigail could've stayed longer, but the light was going and I didn't want her to get caught outside at dusk again. Not even in all her practical, scientist-lady gear.

Never thought I'd find waterproof pants erotic.

"Cain," Griff calls from the ground below, his exasperation loud enough for half the mountain to hear. "Stop fucking about and climb."

Yeah, okay. I shake my head, like I might knock the circling thoughts of Abigail loose, and reach up for my next handhold. This should be a straightforward route, a training drill to keep our skills sharp, and here I am making a meal of it. The other folks from mountain rescue—mostly men but a few women too—are milling around down there, talking quietly as they wait their turn.

The rock is cold but dry. That's good, at least. Nothing worse than climbing up wet, slippery rock. Clumps of moss grow between the cracks, spongy beneath my probing fingers, and I heave myself up another foot.

Not far now.

I'm not a natural climber. More buffalo than mountain goat. But it's part of the job, and I come in handy whenever a big hiker gets hurt and needs to be slung over a broad shoulder, or when a fallen tree needs shoving out the way.

"Aim for that ledge," Griff calls.

I grunt in response and change direction. He wants me to prove I can do the fiddly bit. Fine.

My legs are burning from this climb.

When I first realized yesterday that my visitor was Abigail, that the voice of my bear-spray angel matched the most beautiful woman I'd ever seen, a part of me died inside. I figured there was no chance. Women like that don't look twice at big, hulking brutes like me.

I was short with her, too. All frazzled and cranky.

But she came inside my cabin, didn't she?

"Watch that—" Griff yells, right as I put my weight on a wobbly foothold. It crumbles out beneath me, a shower of rock pieces thundering toward the earth, and I yell "Heads!" as my rope snaps taut.

The breath slams from my body. I swing toward the rock face and kick out just in time, spinning queasily in the air. The sky is thick with clouds.

The rope shudders from the force of my sudden weight, taut enough to pluck like a guitar string, and I hold on with shaking hands. My breaths are loud.

Fuck.

Fuck.

"Everyone okay down there?" There's a chorus of agreement, but Griff is notably silent. Yeah, he'll kick my ass when I'm back on the ground.

I shake my head, digging my raw fingers into my chalk bag and slapping my hands together. Enough mooning around like an idiot.

Time to finish this climb.

* * *

"You've done that route a hundred times, man."

"I know."

"You were all over the place today."

"Yeah, I was. I know."

You'd think that my boss would be pleased that I'm agreeing

with him, not arguing to puff up my wounded ego, but Griff glares at me, his face sour. We're loading up the truck with the climbing gear, the last to leave the training site, and the afternoon wind blows cold against my sweat-damp skin.

It's getting frostier out here. Summer's nearly over.

Will Abigail leave soon? Damn it.

"You're doing it again." Griff heaves a coil of rope into the truck bed, the weight slamming against the metal, and he looks like he wouldn't mind shoving me in there too. "You've gone all dreamy and distant. What the hell, Cain? I need you to be focused."

He's right. Of course he's right.

"I know. Sorry."

The thing is, if we'd been called out for real today, I'd have focused on the rescue, no problem. It's easy to concentrate when there are folks who need us, folks who are scared or in pain. But Griff said it himself—I've done that climb a hundred times, and there were no stakes except getting to the top.

I got sloppy. It's no excuse, but it's the truth.

"You know what? Walk it off." Griff slings the last bag of kit in the truck, then stomps around to the driver's side. He pauses with the door open, one hand gripping the metal. He won't look at me, staring past my shoulder at the trees instead. "I'll take this load to headquarters. Go home, Cain, and… figure it out."

There's a burning sensation in my chest. Like acid trickling between my ribs, because my oldest friend won't look me in the eye.

I really screwed up today.

"Yeah, okay. See you for the late shift tomorrow, then."

The truck dips under Griff's weight, and the slam of the door echoes around the mountainside. My boss peels away down the dirt path, engine growling and truck rocking, like he can't wait to leave me in his dust.

As I watch him go, I scrub a palm over my face, remembering my chalky fingers too late. Now I probably have pale streaks on my cheeks.

Shit.

This is not a proud day. And I've never been like this before, never been tangled up in knots over a woman so badly I can't think, but something about Abigail has messed up my insides. Like someone picking up a box of puzzle pieces and shaking them into a big muddle.

Walk it off, Griff said.

Yeah, okay. Guess I'll try that. It's as good an idea as any.

My insides raw, I turn and head between the trees.

Walk it off.

* * *

I find Abigail in a copse of pine trees partway up the mountain, her binoculars glued to her eyes. Wasn't looking for her, exactly, but now that I've found her, it's like stumbling on buried treasure.

Don't think this is what Griff had in mind.

She's bundled up in her padded green jacket and black fleece leggings, her backpack slumped at her feet, and she's watching a bird flit between the tree branches.

"Woodpecker?" I ask, strolling closer, and I hide a grin when Abigail jumps. She swings around to look at me, pointing those binoculars at my bulk. Lord, I don't want to think about how big I must seem through those. Like Goliath in dark pants and a plaid button down.

"Cain," Abigail gasps, like she's relieved to see me. Like she's pleased.

At least something's going my way today.

I jerk my chin at the tree. "Well?"

"It's a hairy woodpecker," she says, lowering her binoculars at last. Those eyes are so blue, blinking up at me like she's not sure I'm real. The feeling's mutual.

"Him and me both."

"No, that's—" she cuts off, mouth tugging up at the corner. "Oh, I see. Right." A wave of confusion passes over her face, and she points at my cheek. "You've got some…"

"Chalk." God damn it. I scrub my face on my rolled shirt sleeve, and now *my* ears are turning red. "We were climbing earlier. Running drills for mountain rescue."

"Oh, wow. That sounds hard."

I grunt. And if I was smart, if I had my head screwed on right, I'd be trying to impress this woman with everything I have. Telling her about daring rescues and saving the day. Instead, I hear the confession come spilling out of my mouth: "Shouldn't be, but I screwed it up. Nearly splattered myself on the cliff."

Those blue eyes are big as saucers. "Oh, no. What happened?"

The hairy woodpecker is suddenly the most interesting thing I've ever seen, even if it's barely bigger than a pine cone. I stare up into the branches, trying to blot out Abigail's perfect shape in the corner of my eye. "Dunno. Got distracted. No one got hurt, though."

Thank god.

"What were you distracted by?"

I clear my throat. Wrack my brain for a good answer, one that won't make her run away screaming.

The silence stretches between us, turning awkward.

Finally, I'm ready to go and walk into the woods never to return, but a small hand tugs at my sleeve. I look down, surprised.

"You've still got some chalk." My scientist's eyes are warm. "Kneel down for a second."

My bones creak like hell after today's climb, but I do it, knee thudding into the dirt. The impact buzzes through my kneecap.

"Abigail." She's barely taller than me, even with me knelt down. Her auburn hair is braided today, pulled into two separate short bunches, and when she moves, I catch a whiff of green apple. Do I smell bad after working up a sweat?

"I've got it." Her zipper scratches down, and she steps closer. Right up to my front, my climbing musk be damned, as the woodpecker flits between the branches past her shoulder, completely forgotten. My girl swipes at my face with the corner of her jacket, dabbing at me carefully with the fleecy bit inside.

She's awful gentle for someone who gassed me with bear spray, and I bring that up.

"Oh, don't." The best shade of pink's spreading over her cheeks, but she bites back a smile. "Still can't believe I did that. So embarrassing."

Yeah? Well, I can't believe *this.* It's like something from a fever dream, all my longings come to life: being alone in a clearing with this woman, her face about level with mine, her touch soft as she brushes chalk from my cheek. Her zipper catches in my beard, tugging slightly, and I grin as she pouts.

"My big gesture, and I'm screwing it up. Classic Abigail."

"You're not screwing it up." Big gesture? What kind of gesture? My pulse races faster in my throat, and I risk it: "No one fusses over me like this, honey. Except maybe Griff."

An eyebrow lifts. "Griff?"

"My boss." I grin wider when she nods, clearly relieved. "No need to be jealous of that grump, Abigail."

I hear the words after I've said them. After it's too late, and they're hanging between us in the quiet clearing. And I could kick myself for presuming so much, for implying that this woman, the most beautiful, smart, funny woman alive, might actually—

"I *was* a bit jealous, for a second there." Abigail shrugs one shoulder, pressing her lips together like she's still fighting a smile but it's a losing battle. "I won't be, though. Not if you don't like this Griff person that way."

Holy shit.

"I definitely don't." That'd make the barbecue with Luna pretty damn awkward. "Big and bearded isn't my type."

"No?" Abigail's smile finally breaks free, and it's like watching the sunrise. "That's funny, because apparently it's mine."

Fucking hell.

I've forgotten how to breathe.

You know, you can wait to find love almost your whole life, you can get dozens of pep talks from your matchmaker friend, you can daydream about what it might be like to meet someone, but when it finally happens...

"Uh," I say, like an ass.

She waits. I don't elaborate.

Then at last, once I've missed every chance she's given me,

once there's no hope to speak up now: "All sorted." Abigail brushes off her hands and steps back. She's still blushing, but she's focusing on her jacket as she zips it back up, staring at her hands with all her might. "I'm, um. It's nice to see you again, Cain."

Ask her to dinner.

Ask her to marry you.

Say something. Anything, you old fool.

"You too." My voice is hoarse.

Abigail nods, waves, snatches up her backpack, and high-tails it into the trees. Heart thumping, I watch her go.

Abigail

~~~
⚜
~~~

I adjust my headphones, then tap up the volume on my laptop. Gradually, the clink and chatter of this coffee shop fades away, replaced by my whispered memo about the red-naped sapsucker. Tugging my coffee closer, I settle back to listen.

Crap.

Is my voice always this weird? I sound so scratchy.

Wrinkling my nose, I sip from my coffee, then tip my head back with a pleased hum. Caffeine. Yes. Such an underrated cure for a battered heart, and mine is *not* a happy organ. I tossed and turned all night, wondering about Cain. Wondering about what he was thinking yesterday.

My laptop screen is mostly dark, with a small progress bar filling up as the seconds pass. I skip forward by one minute, flinching as the sound of bear spray and Cain's bellow fills my ears. Coffee sloshes over the rim of my mug, trickling down to the table.

Oops.

Skip. Skip.

Here we go. We're walking together, chatting and calm. At least, *I'm* chatting, and Cain is calm. It's so difficult to tell through the recording whether he likes me, whether he's genuinely happy to spend time together, and I huff, raising the volume even higher until my ears buzz with each word.

I was almost certain yesterday—that Cain likes me too. But then I put myself out there and... nothing.

So. More research required.

That's what I'm doing when the woman approaches: dabbing my spilled coffee with a napkin and frowning at my laptop screen, lost to the world in my recording of the first night I met Cain.

"Um. Excuse me?"

It takes me way too long to realize she's talking to me. I'm bordering on rude, but in my defense, strangers hardly ever approach me. My mother used to say I look 'prickly'.

"Excuse me? Could you—could you take the headphones off for a second?"

Definitely talking to me. I slide them onto my neck, already blushing.

"Sorry."

The woman smiles at me, clearly relieved that I'm normal-ish, and I wait for her to say what she wants. Probably to borrow the spare chair from my table.

That's fine. I'm not expecting company.

"Could I join you for a minute?"

I blink. Then nod at her, dazed, as the woman pulls out the seat across from mine, placing her own coffee on the table. It's in a take out cup, but she seems to be getting settled, shrugging off her jacket and plopping down with a sigh.

With her long brown hair and friendly eyes, her baggy green sweater and her wide smile, this is exactly the kind of woman I used to imagine being friends with. The sort of person I could go for walks with, or drop round her place for coffee, or… or do whatever else friends do.

I've been a loner for a long time.

Moving slowly, like I might spook her, I tap a key on my laptop to pause the recording. "Hello. I'm Abigail."

The woman beams even wider. "I thought you might be. I'm Grace. A friend of Cain's."

Just like that, my stomach plummets below the table. Is she warning me off? Is she a real friend, or a *friend* friend? Is this the human version of marking territory? God, woodpeckers are so much simpler.

"He's mentioned you," Grace prompts.

"Yes." I clear my throat, casting around for something innocent to say and coming up blank. "I accidentally got him with a can of bear spray."

Grace snorts. My shoulders relax an inch.

This doesn't feel like a maybe-girlfriend shakedown.

But I have to be sure, and I'm not subtle enough to figure it out another way. "So you and Cain…?"

I'm squeezing the edge of the table like we're on a rocking ship. So weird. Forcing myself to breathe, I unclamp my fingers from the wood and knot them in my lap as Grace says, "Oh! Oh, no. God, no. I'm married to another man. Look, this is Aiden—" a phone screen shoves in my face, with a handsome bearded man splattered with paint "—and this is our son, Benjamin. They're having a boys' day today."

Grace pulls her phone back and smiles, misty-eyed, at the pudgy baby on the screen.

"Cute," I supply, and my new friend nods.

"Super cute."

Nailed it. And I'm building confidence, thinking that maybe I can do this whole friend thing, but then—

"So, Abigail." Grace sips from her coffee before pinning me with a look. "I'm Cain's matchmaker. He's been looking for love for months, and then today, out of nowhere, he fired me. Pulled down his Soulmate Express profile. Any ideas why he did that?"

Um. How should I know?

"Without knowing more about your work performance..." I really miss my woodpeckers. They don't ask me questions with buried landmines. "Sorry. No."

Grace laughs, unoffended, shaking her head. "He said you were a straight talker. And I love that, so I'm wondering if you'll tell me... do you like him? Would you like to date Cain?"

Gah. I scrabble for my coffee mug, and kill time with a long, scalding sip. But what exactly am I hiding from here?

"I already told him that," I say at last, lowering my drink. What's the point in lying? If they're friends, Grace will hear about it eventually, and maybe this is the objective third party input I need. "I said he was my type."

Grace leans forward, and you'd think this is the most intense story she's ever heard. Her eyes are wide, fixed on me, and her grip is tight on her coffee cup. "And?"

"And he said, 'uh.'"

Just reliving it, heat crawls up my neck. The startled look in his eyes; the way his mouth opened then closed. The complete lack of reaction.

Kill me now.

Grace presses her lips together, eyelids fluttering as she sits back. I wait, stomach churning, but she doesn't mention Cain again. She shakes her head, then asks, nice and bright, "Do you like barbecues, Abigail? Are you free on Saturday?"

Um. Sure.

Guess we're on to new topics. Probably for the best, and you know what? I've waited all summer to make friends in this town.

The woodpeckers will be fine without me for one day. The new, sociable Abigail is here.

* * *

The trudge back to my cabin is long, slow and sad. Usually I like walking in the mountains, feeling the fresh air sting my cheeks and the wind ruffle my hair, but today there's a hollow ache where my heart should be, and my shoulders are slumped beneath my backpack straps. Not even the cry of a downy woodpecker overhead in the trees can lift my spirits.

"Female juvenile," I mumble into my phone. "Feeding in a silver birch. Social calls."

Poor little woodpecker. She doesn't know yet that the world will do a number on you.

Because Cain has been looking for love for months. That's what Grace said back there in the coffee shop. He's been actively trying to meet someone, working with Grace at Soulmate Express, and then I all but threw myself at his feet and he still turned me down.

He'd rather date literal strangers than me. I huff, kicking out at a pebble. I'm not *that* bad.

Sure, I'm not glamorous, and when I make people laugh, it's usually accidental. And yes, I'm socially awkward as hell, and when we first met I whammed him with bear spray.

But I'm smart. Hardworking. I cook nutritious meals and I always recycle. I'd be the most loyal, caring girlfriend ever, if he'd only just *see* me—

Nope. Not going down this road.

I have a PhD in ornithology, damn it. The only creatures I'll ever lose my mind over all have feathers.

By the time I reach my cabin, dusk is coming on fast, the shadows of the trees stretching long and deep. My nose is ice cold and I keep sniffling as I walk, feeling wrung out from the hike. It's like between the coffee shop and my door, I've gone through the stages of grief.

"Abigail." A shadow lurches upright on my deck, and I scream. "Abigail! Wait, it's me. It's Cain."

Holy. Shit.

I grip the wooden rail of my cabin steps, wheezing at the ground. My heart's thundering so fast, I'm surprised I'm not juddering like a mechanical toy. "Now," I force out at last, "we're even."

Cain's laugh sounds pained. "So we are." A big hand lands between my shoulder blades, rubbing slow circles through my jacket, and my eyes slam closed.

He's touching me. By choice.

I sniffle. "Cain? What are you doing here?"

"Uh." Huge boots shift against my deck, the wood groaning under his weight. "Came to see you, Abigail."

This man is so confusing. One minute he's brushing me off, then he sits on my cabin steps for god knows how long, waiting for me while the sun goes down.

"I was in the coffee shop."

"Sounds nice." He's still rubbing my back.

"I met Grace. Your matchmaker? She said you fired her today."

Cain grunts, unabashed. "Yeah."

"Why did you fire her?" I swear to all that is feathered, if he doesn't give me a straight answer, one I can make sense of, I'm going to scream again.

But Cain's boots shift again, and then he answers me slowly, like it should be obvious. "I fired her because I met you. Don't need a matchmaker now. Why would I want to meet anyone else?"

Oh my god. The pieces clunk together in my head, a whole day too late.

It's not that he doesn't want me. Cain's awkward too. There's two of us.

…We're doomed.

I stay leaned over for a few seconds longer, schooling my features in the shadows. Breathing steadily until I'm ready to straighten up and be a normal human woman. My stomach's fluttering with a dozen woodpeckers.

"Well, then." Despite all my preparation, I sound strangled. "Aren't you coming inside?"

This is it. Crunch time. The final test.

And Cain grins far above me, his beard shifting in the dark. "Been hoping you'd ask me that again."

Cain

Abigail's rented cabin has a generator. Interesting. She flicks on a table lamp as we enter, the golden light spilling through the room, and I make a mental note to wire up my cabin over the next few weeks.

She won't lose anything by moving in with me—if I ever get that lucky, that is. I won't ever make my scientist slum it. Me, I've always liked firelight and the simple life, but I like making Abigail happy even better.

Electricity. Hot water. Internet. Nightly foot rubs.

She can have it all. Anything she asks of me, I'll make it happen.

"I only have instant coffee or lemon tea."

"Coffee, please."

Watching her bustle around her little kitchen, fetching mugs and boiling water, settles something deep inside me. I'm so calm, being here with Abigail. It's so *right*.

Does she feel it too?

Lord, I hope so. Never wanted anything more in my whole

life.

"I have a theory," Abigail states, addressing the mugs on the counter with a frown. She's stirring my coffee, the steam rising in elaborate curls. "Would you like to hear my hypothesis?"

Probably. "...Yeah?"

An amused smile flickers in my direction, and I wish I could catch it in my fist. Press it over my aching heart.

Abigail sucks in a sharp breath, squaring her shoulders. She looks so small in her kitchen, more birdlike than ever. "You like me, Cain. You'd like to date me, and maybe... maybe more. Eventually. Am I correct?"

Well, yeah. Obviously. That ain't a secret—half the mountain knows already that I'm head over boots for Abigail. But if she needs the confirmation, that's fine by me.

"Yeah, that's right."

The tension floods out of her, my beautiful scientist sagging against the counter, and I realize for the first time how tense she's been. Has she been waiting for me to say it all this time?

I really am an old fool.

Well, better late than never. I stride to meet her in a few steps, rounding the kitchen counter, and take her by the waist. Abigail squawks as I pick her up, settling her beside the steaming mugs, then nudge them both to a safe distance.

Not taking any risks. Not with my girl. She is mine, right?

Her padded green jacket rustles under my hold.

"Oh," Abigail says, and I guess it's her turn to be dumbstruck. I know the feeling well. When she smiled at me and told me she liked 'em big and bearded in that clearing, I nearly died and went to heaven on the spot. "Oh, um. Hello."

"Hi. I've got some notes for your theory."

She nods, suddenly all business. Fuck, I love her so much.

"Go on. I'm all for peer review."

"Okay, here it is. I don't just want you, Abigail: I'm crazy about you. Nearly splattered myself on a rock face yesterday because I couldn't focus, I was so busy thinking about you."

"Well I don't like *that*—" she huffs, but I talk over her, building up steam, squeezing and releasing her padded jacket in my hands.

"You're everything I've been wanting. Everything I've been looking for all these years. And I sure hope you want me too, honey, sure hope you don't mind being with the local Bigfoot, because now that I've met you, no one else will do. If you say no to me, I won't keep looking another day, because I don't want any other. No one else would fit me like you do."

"I'm not sure we *will* fit," Abigail says weakly, capturing one of my hands and spreading her palm over mine. The tips of her fingers barely reach my first knuckles. "Physically, anyway."

Who cares? Sex is the least important bit. "We'll figure it out. If you want us to, Abigail."

She swallows hard, throat working, and pierces me with those baby blue eyes. "Um. Yes, I want to, Cain. If you're—if you're certain about me."

Oh, I'm certain. I'm all-fucking-in.

"Can we start now?" Abigail asks, and my heart lurches. She blinks up at me, shy but determined. Two boots hook around the backs of my legs. "I'm twenty eight years old, you know. I've been wondering what it's like."

Her and me both—except I've got more than a decade on her. Can a skill be rusty if you've never used it once?

"Sure. But I'm a learner driver, Abigail." Her zipper draws down, scratching shakily in the quiet. I tease her jacket off, then toss it over the back of the nearby sofa, and I can't believe

I'm doing this. Can't believe I'm undressing my scientist. Outer layers, but still. "Don't judge the whole activity by the first try, okay?"

She shakes her head, eager and smiling. "Experiments are meant to be repeated."

Fuck. Okay.

This is really happening. I'm—we're—

Abigail cups the side of my face, then draws my mouth down to hers. The moment our lips meet, something detonates in my chest, shock waves rippling through my body. She's so warm, so perfect, so *right.*

I groan, kissing her harder. Plunge my fingers into her silky hair.

Abigail clutches my shirt, breathing heavily, and she gives as good as she gets. Nips my bottom lip and strokes her tongue against mine and ruins me, second by second.

I'm harder than stone in my jeans, my zipper biting into my shaft. I shift between her legs, wincing.

Because what if she's right? What if we can't make it fit? What if I never get inside her? Nerves tighten my throat, and I jolt as slender fingers tug on my belt, working the buckle undone.

"You don't have to," I rasp as Abigail's hand wraps around my cock, pulling me out into the cool air between us. I'm rock hard and ruddy, moisture beading at the tip, and my shaft looks so angry and huge in her hand.

Does she like it? Is she repulsed? God, what does she think?

Pushing her hair out of her eyes, I lean down for a proper look. Abigail gazes back at me, hazy and flushed, her eyes darting down like she can't keep away. She wets her bottom lip, and I choke back another groan.

"Can I lick it?"

This is it: this is how I die.

But what a way to go.

She squeaks, wrapping her arms around my neck as I pluck her off the counter, stomping over to the sofa. I'm clumsy with my jeans undone, shuffling with my stiff cock between us, but Abigail doesn't seem to mind. She sighs happily, pressing kisses along my bearded jaw, and when I sit down with an almighty creak, she wriggles against my lap and gets her hands on me again. I hiss between my teeth, bucking into her gentle grip.

"Pretty sure I need to get *you* ready, not the other way around."

She's staring hypnotized at the shaft in her hands. Running her fingertips all over it, her touch featherlight. "Just for a minute, I promise."

Am I really arguing this? I'd have to be dumber than a box of rocks to tell her no. "Go on, then."

She slithers onto the rug between my knees, shooting me a mischievous grin. And I barely have time to smile back, barely have a chance to brace myself before my scientist ducks her head, her lips sealing around the head of my cock.

My back jerks off the sofa. "Jesus Christ!" Her tongue swirls around the head, hot and torturous, and I thump the arm of the sofa, my stomach coiling tight. "I thought you didn't know what you were doing!"

Abigail pulls off and scoffs, her breath making my nerves tingle. "I said I don't have practical experience. I didn't say I'd never done any research. Come on, Cain."

Ha. Yeah, well that research is about to make a fool of me. I'm rocking into the wet heat of her mouth, mindless and panting, the sofa creaking under my bulk. She sucks as much of me into her mouth as she can handle; she breathes through her nose and bobs her head. Every atom in my body is trembling, tensed, honed in on the perfect torture of her lips and tongue.

"Have mercy." I screw my eyes shut, blood pumping in my ears, and my voice gets more urgent. "Abigail, if you want us to do more tonight—"

She pulls off with a pop, her chin slick in the lamplight. She smiles up at me, so sweetly that I'm dazed. "Yes, I want to do more."

Can't decide whether she's an angel or a little demon. Either way, I love her.

"Stand up, honey. Take your clothes off." Watching her shed her layers, so quick and unpretentious, my throat is too thick to swallow. Fuck, she's perfect under there, all curving hips and pert tits. "Good girl."

Abigail chokes out a laugh, her blush burning bright as she kicks her leggings onto the rug. "I should be offended, I know, but… I like hearing that."

And I like saying it. I like everything about this.

I like the flush spreading over her chest, and the way her pulse is leaping in her throat, and the careful way she crawls back into my lap, like she's scared of kneeling on something vital. I like the way she muffles her squeak against my shoulder as I flip us, laying her down on the sofa cushions, and I like the way her thighs drop open to welcome me, like there's nothing more natural.

I especially like the tiny bird tattoo on her left ankle. I kiss it on my way to lay flat between her legs.

"Take your shirt off," she orders.

"Yes, ma'am." I kneel up and shrug it off, grinning.

The fabric lands with a *thwump* somewhere across the cabin, and yeah, there's something so good about feeling her bare, silky skin against my chest hair. About sharing body heat. It's primal. Slinging her thigh over my shoulder, I lean down and breathe against her slit, my stomach tight with anticipation.

"Um." Abigail squirms beneath me, forehead puckered. "Oh. That's odd."

My stomach drops. "You want me to stop?"

Please say no. Please say no.

And thank god, she shakes her head, her breath stuttering. "No, keep going. I'm just... this is..."

I pat her thigh, trying to find the right words to comfort her beautiful brain. "Gather your data, honey." A beaming smile tells me I've hit the jackpot. "I'll stop whenever you've had enough."

It's gonna have to be that way, because *I'll* never be done. Not with the sight of her puffy lips, glistening and pink, and not with the salty sweet taste that greets my tongue. Not with the way her breath catches, body arching against the sofa cushions, or the way her heel digs into my back, urging me on as I lick her deeper, then lap at her clit.

And the sounds she makes. The goddamn sounds.

We're gonna have to record one of the little voice notes she told me about someday. I want these breathy moans on demand.

After a minute or two, I say: "I'm going to add a finger."

Her stomach trembles. "Okay."

I lick her through it, soothing as best I can. And though she's tensed up like a little statue, my finger slides in easy, nice and slick. Her body sucks me in, welcoming and warm, and I grit my teeth against the bolt of pure lust arrowing through my gut.

"Oh," Abigail sighs, melting against the cushions. "Oh, I see."

By the time I add a second finger, she's mewling. Rocking her hips up, rubbing herself over my mouth, my fingers crooking inside her. So shameless and sweet.

"Cain," she gasps, her heel digging into my back. "Cain, I'm ready now. Quickly. Do it quickly."

No, we're not rushing this part—but I do give her one last lick, and draw my fingers out. Then push over her, taking in every detail of her mussed hair and pink cheeks and electric blue eyes.

I notch myself against her entrance—and wince at the size difference.

"You sure about this?" If I hurt her... if I get this wrong...

Abigail smooths her palms over my chest, and her smile is so full of trust. "I'm sure. Just—go gently."

"I will."

The cabin is silent. Our breaths are labored, coming hard.

I squeeze my eyes shut and push inside.

Abigail

❧⧼◌∽◌⧽❧

Well, I can't say I wasn't warned. Everything about Cain, from his nickname to his hands to his deep, rumbling voice, told me that he'd probably be big all over. And fine, I'll admit it—ever since I met him, I've wondered what that might be like. Feeling a big, thick shaft pushing inside me.

Turns out: it's a lot.

"Slower," I gasp, even though Cain's already pressing forward at a glacial pace, his muscles tense and shuddering with restraint. A tendon stands out on his neck, half buried by his dark beard, and I focus on that, zooming in every ounce of my attention on the salt and pepper dusting his jaw. He's a very distinguished sasquatch. "Okay. Okay. Keeping going."

Cain grunts, his eyes screwed shut.

And I know it's messed up, but I love his caveman noises. They make me feel all warm and glowy in my chest, and I bite hard on my bottom lip as he growls and sinks another inch inside me.

It's a *stretch*. And it burns where his body meets mine, but it's not painful, exactly. It's not unpleasant.

I mostly feel... full. And getting fuller.

"Cain," I whimper, dragging his shoulders closer.

"Yeah, honey." His big, bristly face rubs against my neck. "Yeah, I'm here."

He eases off. Pushes forward. Eases off, pushes forward, working himself inside me so patiently, inch by careful inch. And every time, it feels impossible that I could fit anymore, that there could even *be* more to come, and yet every time, I take it.

I take it, and it feels...

Incredible.

How strange that I've never felt more powerful than with this bearded giant lying on top of me, his shaft splitting me in two. But my body is flushed and my skin is damp with sweat and I can't stop squirming, sighing, *wanting.*

I'm coming alive.

It's heady. Especially when Cain pushes up to get a good look at me, his eyes crinkling with relief when he sees how much I love this. How much I want more.

"You okay down there, honey?"

I clamp down on his cock, and he groans. "Yes, thank you."

Cain shakes his head, shoulders quaking as he rumbles with laughter. And I can feel all those vibrations buzzing through my bloodstream; can feel his pulse where he's speared inside me. We're so tightly sealed, without an inch between us, and for the first time in years, I shrug off my loneliness like a damp towel.

Feels good. Toasty warm.

"Ah, hell. Abigail." Cain's moving now, thrusting gently

between my legs, then snapping his hips harder when I urge him on. "Your body. Your perfect body. You have no idea how good this feels."

I think I have *some* idea. Every time Cain presses inside me again, a shower of sparks bursts through my insides.

"Been waiting for you for so long. Been worried you'd never show."

I wrap my arms tighter around Cain's neck, burying my face in his bristly throat. His skin is damp and feverish, and tastes salty when I lick it. "I'm here now."

"And you're staying." He says it like an order, but there's a silent question under there. My nod makes him curse and thrust harder. "You're mine, honey. I'm gonna make you so happy, I swear."

He already has. Already does.

"I believe you."

Cain groans, reaching one hand between us to palm my breast, and though his movements are clumsy, the sheer size of his hand on me is enough to make my toes curl. He's so huge, and husky, and pure man.

Blunt fingers pinch my nipple. My thighs tighten on his waist, stomach clenching, and my whimper makes Cain grin.

"Felt good, huh?"

Oh, yes. "Do it again."

This is how we learn each other: with muttered questions and commands. With shared laughter and the slick slide of our bodies. The sofa creaks beneath our shared weight and the windows are pitch black, but we don't stop, and I don't get cold beneath Cain's strong body and warm skin.

He's thick. Muscled and hairy, with a big slab of a stomach, and two arms like tree trunks. When he plunges between my thighs, it's like he'll never get close enough; like he's chasing heaven. His belt buckle clinks somewhere below his hips, and he's still half-wearing his jeans.

Next time I'll get him fully naked. Or maybe I'll get my mouth on him again, and suck him past all those garbled warnings. See what happens then—for science.

"Gonna come inside you, Abigail."

My breath catches. Yes—that. I want that.

"Gonna come soon, honey. Are you close?"

Am I close? I bite my lip and close my eyes, cataloging the sensations in my body. I'm burning hot and can't keep still; there's a knot of tension in my lower body that feels impossibly tight. Every thrust drives me higher, up to an invisible ledge, and when Cain pinches my nipple again, I go still, muscles twitching.

"Gah!" It takes over me without warning, buffeting me in a storm of sensation. I'm rigid beneath Cain, clamped down tight on his shaft; my ears pop and my teeth clench. Wave after wave thunders through me, stealing my breath and making me moan, and when I finally slump back against the sofa cushions, I feel like I've run ten miles.

"Jesus," Cain mutters, pushing up onto his knees and gripping my thighs. He keeps thrusting, his eyes wide as he watches our bodies meet. "You could've warned me, Abigail. Nearly died on top of you just then."

My laugh is strangled. "How could I have known?"

His beard shifts as he grins, but then his eyes slam shut and the smile drops away. Cain's silent, almost serious as he stills above me, wet warmth blooming in my core. Sealing all our promises.

"Abigail," he says a moment later, and my name sounds like

an oath. My Bigfoot shakes his head, blinking down at me with awe. "That was…"

Yeah. It really was.

I pat his hairy forearm. "An excellent first experiment. To be repeated as soon as conditions allow."

Cain throws back his head and roars with laughter.

* * *

We walk up the path to the cabin together, and though I don't mention my nerves, Cain must sense them, because he captures my hand in his big paw.

"They're good people, honey. And they're going to love you. Grace invited you, didn't she?"

"Yes," I agree, privately wrestling with my doubts. I'm being silly. Why would she invite me to a private barbecue if she didn't want to be friends?

There are steps leading up to the cabin, and a wraparound deck, but Cain leads me around the side like he's been here dozens of times before. I stare openly at the wood store as we pass with its carefully sheltered pile of cut logs, a stack of blank canvases stored at its side.

Does Grace paint? No—that photo of her husband, Aiden, showed him splattered with color. What was her baby's name again?

Oh, god. I can't do this.

Cain squeezes my hand. "Ten minutes, okay? And if you hate it, we'll leave."

Ten minutes. Yes, okay. I can survive ten minutes.

The thing is, I'm awkward at the best of times, but now there are stakes to this barbecue. I'm meeting Cain's friends; seeing if they could like me. And if they don't, where does that leave us?

"Okay, wait a second." Cain tugs me to a halt before we round the last corner of the cabin, the sounds of the barbecue already drifting to us on the crisp fall air. There's the gentle strum of a guitar, and a burst of quick, feminine laughter. The crackle of a fire and the clink of glass bottles. Chatter. Comfort. Friends. "You're tenser than a plank of wood. Should we leave and pretend we never came?"

I shake my head fast, chin wobbling. "No, I can do this. But if they don't like me, Cain…"

"They will," he says, so confident, and kneels down right there on the frozen ground. With our faces level, his crumples with concern. "Why are you so stressed about this? You're a smart, funny, interesting person. Of course they'll love you, but if they don't… well, fuck 'em."

A startled laugh bursts out of me. "Fuck them?"

"Yeah. If they don't like you, they must have terrible taste."

"They're your friends, Cain."

"And you're my woman." He grins at my eye roll. "Don't pretend you don't like it when I call you that. I know you like a bit of caveman, Abigail. Now, come on." His knees crack as he pushes to his full, impressive height and takes my hand again. "I want to show you off to Griff. Make him see why I couldn't do a simple climb."

My heart flutters as we round the cabin. Grace turns and spots us, and I smile nervously at her wave. "I don't think that's a valid excuse."

"Wait until we're over there before you throw me under the bus, honey. Griff will love that."

As we approach, Grace's eyes drop to our joined hands,

then she lets out an almighty whoop, thumping a black-haired woman beside her on the shoulder. "Nina!"

A blond man prods at the fire pit with a long stick. "Please don't punch my pregnant wife. I'll have to get out of my seat."

"Shut up, Merrick," the woman called Nina says. "*Look.*"

As one, the whole party turns to stare. There's Nina and Grace and the man I recognize as Aiden from her phone. The sarcastic Merrick, and a silvery haired woman, perched on another bearded man's knee. Griff, I assume.

Only the baby is unbothered by our arrival. He's curled against Aiden's shoulder, a dark patch of drool spreading over the man's gray shirt.

"Benjamin!" His name bursts out of me, and my steps are lighter once I've remembered. "Hi, Benjamin."

Grace sidles over to her husband as we join the group, elbowing him in the ribs. "The perfect record continues."

"Not sure you get credit for this one," Aiden rasps, and his throat sounds terribly painful, but he offers a small smile in welcome.

Grace scoffs. "I coached Cain for months! And when he told me about Abigail, I helped him figure out his pitch."

My Bigfoot smiles down at me, sheepish. "We won't tell her how badly I did. Okay?"

"Deal."

It doesn't take long for the chatter to start up again, or for Cain and I to be absorbed into the group. They're funny and welcoming and even when I say exactly the wrong thing, they all grin over my head at Cain, so visibly pleased that I'm here.

It's... a lot.

But it's very nice.

"Ten minutes are up," a bristly mouth murmurs in my ear.

"Want to stay a bit longer?"

I suck in a deep breath and glance around the barbecue, at the fire pit and the loose circle of seats. The grill heating up to one side and the cooler of sodas and beers. The laughing guests and their relaxed smiles, all except the baby sleeping on Aiden's shoulder.

It's an easy decision really.

"Yes. I want to stay."

Cain

❧

Three years later

I find my wife on the new deck I built her two summers ago, rocking in her favorite chair. She's swaddled in thick blankets, our daughter cradled against her chest, and a cold mug of lemon tea sits on a stool by her side, forgotten.

I ruffle her auburn hair once I reach her side. "See anything good?"

Abigail nods slightly, her binoculars held to her face with one hand. "There's a red-naped sapsucker in that silver birch."

I grunt. "My favorite."

My wife lowers her binoculars and beams up at me. "Mine too."

I flip the blankets back, getting a better view at the pink-faced baby smushed against her chest. It's probably too early to tell, but I think our daughter takes after her mother's looks. Probably for the best. "Has she been good?"

"Yes." Abigail shifts, gathering up the baby, and lifts her toward me. I'm greeted with bleary eyes and a soft gurgle. "But she misses her dad."

Ah, hell. An old fool like me shouldn't feel this much emotion in one go. If I'm not careful, it'll fell me like a tree, but I still cradle my daughter against my chest; I still kiss her soft head and gaze down at my wife.

They're everything to me. Everything.

"You want a fresh tea?"

Abigail blinks at her abandoned drink, clearly having forgotten it was there. "Oh. Yes, I suppose so. Yes, please. And, um. Could I have one of those toffee pecan cookies with it?"

Yes she fucking can. This woman has given me the whole goddamn world.

I shift my baby higher against my chest. "Lemon tea and a cookie. You got it."

Anything my scientist wants, she'll get.

This Bigfoot knows how to spoil his woman.

* * *

Thank for reading the Mail Order Mountain series! I hope you loved it. :)

For more cozy instalove stories, check out the Winter Warmers! *An ice skating coach and a fabled man in the woods. A gruff clockmaker and a snowed-in duke...*

And for a bonus instalove story, grab your copy of Ride or Die. *She's sweet and innocent—and that's like catnip in this strip club. It's okay, though. I won't let the pretty bartender out of my sight.*

Happy reading!

xxx

Teaser: *Cold Wood*

There are plenty of downsides to being universally hated. To starring in little kids' nightmares and playing the role of the local bogeyman. There's the shame and self loathing, obviously. The loneliness that burrows down into my marrow, freezing me from the inside out. Not to mention the *boredom.*

But there are positives, too—like having the woods all to myself, and not answering to anyone else. Like minding my own damn business. It's peaceful.

Most of the time, anyway.

But not tonight. Tonight, some girl won't stop screaming. And I'm not in the fucking mood.

It's probably a bunch of schoolkids, coming out here on a dare. Winding each other up, and trying to see who cries first. But it's getting dark, the moon shining between the bruised clouds, and those little shits will find more trouble than they're looking for if they stay in these woods after nightfall.

The wolves are hungry at this time of year. The bears, too. Hell, we're *all* hungry. The scream wails louder, and I heft my ax, adjusting my grip on the handle as I stride through the trees. A small deer hangs over my shoulder, body cooling and head lolling against my back, and my boots drum against the ground, pine needles trembling over the dirt.

Damn it, I should be heading home. Back to my cabin in the deepest part of the woods, to skin and treat my dinner—not chasing after some foolish schoolkids who came looking for me on a dare.

I hate that goddamn town. Those stupid stories. How would they like it? How would they like being called a monster, all because of some scars?

The screams get louder, rising in pitch as I approach, high and terrified. I weave through the trees, my grip tight on my ax as unease slithers through my gut. I may be sick to death of the locals daring each other to sneak into my woods, but that doesn't mean I want anyone *hurt.* Far from it.

They'd never use me as a scary story if they knew the truth about me. I'm a teddy bear. A huge, scarred, angry-looking one, but a teddy bear all the same.

I hear the wolves before I see them. They're snarling, snapping their teeth, hurling themselves into the air and landing with a crash. And when I peer through the trunks, I see what's got them in a frenzy: there's a crimson bundle, clinging to the top branches of a tree.

"Hey!"

The wolves know my voice after all these years. They're my neighbors, basically; they know more about me than the people in that town. So they know I mean business when I stride into view, ax raised, deer carcass listing to the side on my shoulder, and they're smarter than the kid up that tree, because they turn and snarl at me, but they don't try anything.

Fur bristling and eyes gleaming, the wolves size me up. They're wondering: could we take him this time?

No they could not. I know it and *they* know it, same as they know not to take on a bear.

"Be careful!" A hoarse female voice floats down from the tree. I ignore it, still staring at the biggest wolf.

"Get on with you." I take a step closer, puffing up my chest and making myself big. Or let's face it—*bigger*. The wolves back up a few feet, snarling, drool dripping between their teeth. I juggle the deer on my shoulder to keep from dropping it, and four sets of eyes land on my dinner.

… Shit.

I flex my grip on the deer's leg. Ah, hell. I was looking forward to this. I was going to make a pie.

The sigh that gusts out of me—it's exhausted. I'm full up to my eyebrows with this nonsense. First they call me a monster, then they cost me my food. I'll have to hunt again tomorrow, and lord knows I take no pleasure in the act.

The girl whimpers above me in the tree.

"Alright, fine."

I stride between the trees, the wolves' muzzles following my path. I don't go far—just far enough to put some distance between me and them. And when I let the deer carcass slide to the forest floor, their tails are practically wagging.

"Come on then, you bastards." I walk a wide arc back to the girl's tree, giving them space to run over there. They streak through the gloom, all flashing teeth and bunching muscles, and then they lay into the deer with low snarls and the crunch of bone.

"Ew," I hear faintly, up in the branches.

Yeah, she got that right. *Ew.* And that would've been her, crunched up like that. I'd like to pretend my own table manners are better than the wolves', but after all these years, I'm not so

233

sure.

Still, I'm all she's got right now, so I tip my head back and peer at the crimson bundle.

"It won't keep them busy forever," I call. My voice is rough, gravelly from hardly ever speaking to another soul. But I know she understands me; I can hear it in the way her breath catches as she clings tighter to the branch, the wind whipping her to and fro.

I wait for a moment. Wait a bit longer.

Nothing.

Not a damn thing. Not even a *thank you.*

"You want me to leave you up there?" After all this time, it shouldn't hurt, but there's an ache in my gut. She thinks I'm a fate worse than hungry wolves? Really? "Suit yourself." I'm turning on my heel before she calls down to me, voice high and clear.

"Wait. Please. I can't—I can't get down."

* * *

I frown, peering up at her. She's wearing some big red hood, and with the fading light, I can't make out her face.

"You got yourself up there just fine."

She huffs. "Well, up is easier than down."

"No, it's not."

"Yes, it is!"

I grunt. "Says who?"

"Says a person of normal height!" I cock my head, trying to size up her balled-up form as she blathers on. "*You* might be able to just step out of the trees, mister, but for us normal folks, this is *very* high up."

Her voice goes all squeaky on that last part. That's how I know she's really frightened. I forgot for a second there, what with her acting so brave.

"How'd you even get up there?" I cross my arms, trying to picture it, my ax dangling from my fingers. Not far away, the wolves are snapping and growling, tearing the deer carcass apart, but it's her I'm focused on. She's so damn high. She's practically clinging to the tippy-top branch, swaying in the wind.

"Adrenaline," she snaps. She's trying to feel her way down, sending out one foot as a scout. She's doing it all wrong.

"They chased you up there like a squirrel."

"I made a *tactical decision.* It was this or be eaten." She blows out a long breath. "Are you going to help me down or not?"

My eyebrows shoot up my forehead. I'm not standing here being deliberately slow—it just never occurred to me that she'd let me put my hands on her. Not with the wolves distracted and the risk of death put off for a few minutes. I figured she'd probably rather them than me.

I reach up for her, then curse and drop my ax, cheeks burning. It lands with a *thunk,* and I scrub my dirty palms over my shirt front, then reach up for her again.

"Uh. Here."

It takes some doing, some fumbling and muttered curses, but the girl in the tree works her way close enough to reach for me instead. She's still above me, wobbling on a gnarled branch, and when she crouches, aiming for my shoulders, that's all the warning I get.

"*Oof.*" Her body slams into mine, knocking the air from my lungs. But I don't even sway back an inch—that's how much smaller she is. I lower her carefully, my hands squeezing her ribs, and I place her down on the carpet of pine needles like she's made of glass.

My heart's pounding a mile a minute in my chest. I can't remember the last time I touched another human being. My fingers are tingling.

"Thank you," she mutters. Like she didn't nearly just give me a heart attack.

I wait for her to take off running, but she stays right there, staring up at me. And when she shrugs her hood back, the earth tilts under my feet.

It's not a girl. Definitely not a child. It's a *woman.* A beautiful young woman, with raven black hair and serious gray eyes, her pretty mouth pressed in a wry smile.

A woman who doesn't even flinch when the wolves snarl louder, fighting over the deer nearby, snapping their jaws and tearing at the meat.

I nod at the carnage over her shoulder. "You should go on home or you'll be dessert."

She snorts. "No kidding. I'm not far away."

No? She lives in the woods, then? There are a few cottages clustered within a mile of the treeline, but I keep my distance from those. I don't want to be seen; don't want to fuel the rumors. It explains how she managed to get caught out on the path, though.

I'm stupidly pleased that she wasn't out on a dare, looking to torment me. Maybe she's not like the others.

But—

"You're him, aren't you?" My heart sinks as she speaks. She inches closer to me, excitement burning in her big eyes. "You're the man in the woods."

I exhale, gusting out all my foolish hopes. "Could be. I'm a man. I'm in the woods."

I know exactly what she means, but I'm sure as hell not going to admit it. I won't claim the stories they make up about me, no way. They talk about me like I'm some baby-eating ogre.

That's who she thinks I am? Even after I helped her? Fuck this. Fuck *her.*

"Get on with you." My voice comes out harsh, but I'm angry now. Fed up and hungry, and damned ashamed at how my body lit up when I held her. Even minutes later, my blood's rushing faster and my muscles are tensed and quivering. Yearning for more. And meanwhile, she thinks I'm some freak, just like everyone else. "If the wolves corner you again, I won't help you. Do you hear me?"

The girl nods, backing up a step. She doesn't look scared, though. She looks thoughtful.

"What's your name?" she asks before she's swallowed up by the trees. Does she know the way home from here? What if she gets lost again? It's a frosty night.

"Blaise," I tell her without thinking, too busy worrying over whether she'll run into a bear. "Hey, how far is your cottage?"

The girl in red chuckles. "I thought you didn't care?"

My pulse is racing as she turns and melts into the darkness, one final flash of crimson before she's gone.

I walk up and down for a few hours as night falls, replaying the feel of her in my arms, ears straining for her voice. Just in case.

* * *

Check out Cold Wood and more snowy goodness in the Winter Warmers collection!

xxx

Cassie Mint

About the Author

Cassie writes outrageous, OTT instalove with tons of sugar and spice. She loves cookie dough, summer barbecues, and her gorgeous cat Missy.

You can connect with me on:

🌐 https://www.authorcassiemint.com
📘 https://www.facebook.com/cassiemintauthor
🔗 https://www.bookbub.com/authors/cassie-mint

Subscribe to my newsletter:

✉ https://www.authorcassiemint.com/newsletter